The House across the Road and other Stories

Dave Schwartz

For Jenni!

Table of Contents

Dedication

-For Diana

June 10, 2007

Did I mention?

I am glad that you are not here today.
I think I am going to tell everyone I see.

Yep!

Good for me.

Me.

I am sooo going to do stuff today!
And NO! I am not going to tell you about any of it.

You.

You will just have to wait…
I am afraid…

Oh! I almost forgot to mention,
After you left.
I found a perfectly empty space in the center of my room.

If it suits me
I may decide to sit there
Enjoying myself
Enjoying your not being here today.

If it suits me…
It is such a perfectly empty space.

Did I mention?

The Prettiest Piglet

In a pretty little valley, surrounded by pretty little mountains, and next to a pretty little stream that ran down from those pretty little mountains, there was a pretty little farm. And on that pretty little farm lived a pretty little piglet named Gwendolyn.

Gwendolyn liked being pretty and she liked being told she was pretty. What Gwendolyn didn't like was being a piglet.

"You are such a pretty piglet!" everyone said. Gwendolyn knew it was true, but she did not like hearing the customary end of that compliment, "piglet"; she didn't like being reminded.

"You are going to be a pretty pig, like your mom," some animals also said. She knew her mom was pretty, but she didn't want the other part to be true. She didn't want to grow up and be a pretty pig. She just wanted to be pretty.

"Why do I have to be a pig when I grow up?" she would think to herself, so she couldn't be heard, in a very loud voice. "I'm prettier than my mom!"

Gwendolyn worked hard to always look pretty. Beginning with the basics that her mother showed her, she became very good at applying makeup to her already pretty face. She would use a little makeup if she wanted to simply highlight how pretty she was. Or she would use a lot of makeup if she wanted to exaggerate her beauty.

And, depending on where she was going and who she might be seeing, or, more importantly, who might be seeing her, she could be very clever with her makeup. She could adjust her eyebrows and the makeup around her eyes in a way that pulled you in and kept you looking at her pretty face. She could make her face look fun, or serious, or adventurous, or silly, or happy, or all of those qualities at once. And no matter how she looked, she was always the prettiest piglet.

One morning, after breakfast, as they were walking away from the trough, her father, a very handsome pig in his own right, noticed pretty, piglet Gwendolyn.

"My dear daughter," he said, "You look absolutely delightful this morning."

It was true. That morning she had painted her face with the intention of looking delightful.

"Why," her father continued, "I'd bet you are the prettiest little piglet I've ever seen on this whole farm."

Her handsome father trotted away to roll in some fresh, soft mud.

"Of course!" she thought to herself loudly so no one could hear her. "The whole farm! It's full of animals. I don't have to be a pig. I can be anything I want, and I can still be the prettiest."

Gwendolyn truly meant it. Except that she said, "I mean it," defiantly, but in a whisper so no one would hear her.

The next morning she woke up early and decided she was going to be a chicken. She had always liked feathers. And so, she put on her makeup and a pretty, green dress covered with pink watermelon slices, that Gwendolyn looked pretty wearing, and she went over to the henhouse to be a chicken.

Realizing she was much too big to be a chick, she went to where the hens had gathered. They had been quietly chatting, gossip mostly, and pecking around the yard for their breakfast. When Gwendolyn walked over, there was a lot of fussing and flapping of feathers. All of the hens were excitedly introducing themselves to her, and Gwendolyn was excitedly introducing herself back.

There were more than a few, "You are such a pretty hen," and Gwendolyn always returned the compliment, whether it was true or not. She never thought it was true.

The hens adored Gwendolyn. She always seemed to be smiling. And her eyebrows framed her bright eyes and that let you know that she was really listening. Gwendolyn was almost never really listening.

That first morning Gwendolyn followed the hens' every move. She asked a lot of chicken questions, and she listened, intently. She was learning everything she could about being a chicken. She couldn't let them know she was really a piglet. She went to bed exhausted, and she slept soundly that first night.

The next morning when Gwendolyn woke up, the other hens were already up quietly chatting, mostly gossip, and pecking about the yard. When she joined them, the hens were just as excited to see her as they had been the morning before. Gwendolyn loved the attention.

The next few days went much the same. She followed the hens

around, did what they did, and talked about the things that they talked about, gossip mostly.

The hens, as I said before, adored Gwendolyn. She always looked so pretty and so happy, and she was fun to be around. And they all became good friends. One day Gwendolyn decorated the henhouse with a wreath she had made of straw and thistle. Another morning she filled a basket with grubs and fresh berries as a surprise treat for all the gals. She had made the basket out of straw and thistle. The hens loved her and paid her wonderful compliments all day long. They admired how pretty she always looked and what a sweet friend she was. Gwendolyn loved being the prettiest hen and having hen friends.

She quickly settled into hen life and one night, not long after she first arrived, she did not go to bed quite so exhausted because she hadn't really learned anything new about being a hen that day. The next morning, she woke up earlier than usual to a very strange sound. The other hens had heard it too and were beginning to gather in the yard.

"You can always count on Rooster. It's exactly sunrise," her friend, Shelly said.

Gwendolyn saw that Shelly was fawning as she talked about Rooster. All of the hens were fawning over Rooster.

When Rooster crowed again, Gwendolyn looked up where all of her fawning hen friends were looking. And there he was.

Rooster was high on top of the barn, and strutting. When he puffed out his chest to crow and announce the new day, the hens went crazy. Gwendolyn found that she too was fawning over Rooster.

"I want to do that," she said out loud.

She imagined herself strutting high on the barn, chest puffed out, announcing the day, all the hens looking up at her, a fawning crowd of admirers.

That night Gwendolyn didn't sleep. She worked through the night on her makeup because she very much wanted to enchant Rooster. And in the morning when she was ready, she was one enchanting hen.

Just before dawn Gwendolyn climbed up to where Rooster was, atop the barn. He saw her strutting over to him and he saw that her makeup was enchanting. But Rooster would have rather spent the last twenty minutes before he had to go to work and crow, as he always had, deliberately drinking his coffee alone. But here was Gwendolyn.

"I just love listening to you! You are so talented! I want to try! Will you teach me?" She was extremely enchanting.

"No," said Rooster ignoring how enchanting Gwendolyn was.

And then he said, "If you don't mind, I need to prepare." Rooster turned his back on her completely and returned to sipping his coffee.

Gwendolyn returned to the other hens. She was with them when Rooster crowed and they all fawned. She didn't fawn. Her feelings had been hurt and she was mad, and she didn't like Rooster at all. The hens didn't notice that she wasn't quite as chipper that morning because her enchanting makeup blended into her sad face and became a pleasant smile.

The next morning Gwendolyn woke up late. The hens were already pecking, and gossiping, mostly. Seeing them she decided she didn't like them much anymore. She realized that they only had two legs each. Gwendolyn had four legs.

"Surely four legs are better than two," she thought silently so no one could hear her.

Gwendolyn knew she could never live as a pretty hen. She needed to be pretty and four-legged. Only four-legged folks could truly understand her. All day she pretended to be a happy, pretty hen. But inside she was imagining what it might be like to be the prettiest on four legs.

That night, when all the hens were sleeping, she snuck out of the henhouse and back to the pig pen where she rolled in mud and ate from the trough and quietly rooted around all by herself. The next morning, she was the prettiest hen again, and the chickens were none the wiser.

Around mid-morning, a dog came bounding through the yard, frightening, and scattering all the chickens. Gwendolyn, trying not to laugh at the hens' distress, was taken with the dog's speed, and its smooth, shiny yellow coat. For a moment she imagined being a pretty dog. When at once, the dog heard its name being called and it obediently turned and ran back to the farmhouse. Every thought of being a pretty dog disappeared. The dog obeyed a command and Gwendolyn definitely did not like doing what she was told.

After she decided that she didn't want to be a pretty dog, Gwendolyn spent the rest of the day by herself, unhappy with being a pretty hen, and coming up with all sorts of things she didn't like about it. She hated the food. It had no flavor. And she hated chicken feathers that got all over everywhere and couldn't help chickens fly anywhere. She wouldn't even consider egg laying. That was something that Gwendolyn didn't think was ever pretty. However, seeing the dog had given her an idea. And the next morning she woke up early, even before Rooster, put on new makeup, and left the henhouse for good, as a pretty cat.

Gwendolyn had long admired the cats. They seemed to be able to do whatever they wanted to do and go wherever they wanted to go. Sometimes they were alone. And sometimes they were together. They only talked if they felt like it. And they were constantly grooming themselves. She liked all of those things about the cats. When she was a hen, Gwendolyn recalled when a cat had raided the henhouse, terrorizing everyone, and sending useless feathers flying. That had made her smile.

Cats were cool and now Gwendolyn was going to be a pretty cool cat. When she had been putting on her makeup, she recalled that when she was a very young piglet, she had learned to mimic the slow confident stride of the cool farm cats. She was walking that way when she sauntered over to three cool cats loafing in the shade and not saying a word. Again, she was too large to be a kitten, so she decided to start as a cat.

At first, the three cool cats sat there indifferently, loafing. But, when Gwendolyn licked her front paws and stuck her curly tail straight up in the air, the cool cats leaped up excitedly and went over to meet the new cool cat.

"Such a pretty girl," they purred and rubbed against her. "Such a pretty kitty."

Gwendolyn and the cool cats spent the day getting to know each other and becoming fast friends. There was bottom scratching, and biscuit making, head butting, low impact wrestling, and they loafed everywhere they felt like it, all around the farm. When they all parted for the night, Gwendolyn couldn't believe how close they had all become so quickly. She loved her cool cat friends.

"They get me. They really, really get me. They even wear makeup just like I do."

Gwendolyn didn't say it, or even think it, exactly. But she did feel it and she fell asleep feeling every bit the prettiest kitty. The next morning she put on her face and then cool, pretty kitty, Gwendolyn, went out to find breakfast and her cool cat friends.

She didn't exactly know where breakfast would be, but she did remember that when she was a piglet she had gotten yelled at for eating a delicious bowl of food that had been freshly set out on the back porch of the farmhouse. She remembered being smiled at and told, "Pretty piglet. That's not for you. That's for the kitties, silly, pretty girl," before being shooed away by a broom. And so off sauntered Gwendolyn, to the back porch of the farmhouse.

When she got there it was too late. The cool cats had already eaten all the food and they were casually licking their paws and grooming themselves. They also completely ignored her. Their makeup was perfect.

"Hey there cool cats."

Without even a glance in her direction, the cool cats were ignoring Gwendolyn and each other.

"Say buddies, is there any more breakfast?"

Not a sound from the cats, who wouldn't say a word or acknowledge each other that entire day.

Gwendolyn was very hungry, but she didn't know what to do. She was quite new at being a cat. She thought about it and didn't think she would look very pretty hunting and eating mice. Besides, even though her toenails were neatly painted, they weren't quite long enough or sharp enough for killing. That night she went to bed very hungry.

The next morning, her hunger woke her up early, even before Rooster, and she was sitting, waiting politely at the back porch door of the farmhouse when the full food dish appeared. Gwendolyn couldn't contain her excitement when she saw and smelled the canned food swimming in its own gravy.

"Oh, you pretty, pretty kitty. Where did you come from?" She heard the farmer say.

"You look famished, poor thing. Let me bring you a big dish of food just for you." Gwendolyn could barely stand still, hopping from paw to paw and rubbing up against the farmer's legs as he went back inside.

When he returned, the farmer set a new dish down in front of Gwendolyn, scratched her head, told her what a pretty kitty she was and then, went off to the barn. The other cool cats, arriving for breakfast, saw how cool and pretty Gwendolyn looked eating from her very own bowl, and they all became very excited to see her.

After they had all eaten a big breakfast, the cool cats spent the day just as they had done the day before yesterday, when they first met Gwendolyn, as best friends. When she said good night to her cool cat friends, she was tired, but she wasn't hungry. Gwendolyn fell asleep quickly.

The next morning she woke up, found her food dish, and ate. But she couldn't find any of the other cats all day, no matter where on the farm she went.

The day after that the cats were there during breakfast, but they were ignoring her again.

And the day after that they were all good friends.

And the day after that they had all disappeared.

Before she knew it, Gwendolyn didn't like being a cool cat, and she found herself regularly sneaking back into the pigpen to root around in the dirt late at night, secretly, so no one would see her.

"I don't think cats are very nice. I want them to like me all the time. Sometimes they just seem mean," she thought to herself. "The hens liked me all the time. I don't know what to expect from the cats."

Gwendolyn was becoming more and more bored pretending to be a cool cat. She didn't like the cats anymore, even when they did tell her what a pretty kitty she was. And so, one morning, she woke up and put on her most ordinary makeup. She was still a pretty kitty, but it was subtle pretty kitty makeup, that, along with her cat-like finesse, wouldn't attract notice as she roamed freely about the farm and gathered information.

That night, as Gwendolyn was falling asleep, she thought about everything she had observed that day. She learned that she didn't want to be a dairy cow because they seemed to only serve others. She didn't want to spend her life serving. Furthermore, and what she truly couldn't understand is how they could all be so happy serving others when there was no reward for it.

Gwendolyn knew that she could never be an owl or a crow or an eagle. No matter how much makeup she put on, it would never be enough to make her fly. Besides, flying birds thought themselves too noble and didn't care much for makeup and those who wore it. They are much too direct in their manner of speech, like Rooster had been. She would never get pretty words from their like.

Gwendolyn ignored the mice. She didn't want to think about being so vulnerable all the time.

She discovered that the sheep were slow and boring, and they all dressed alike, and the rams were elitists. Gwendolyn wanted excitement and understanding.

Being around the horses had made Gwendolyn uncomfortable. They were beautiful and when they moved, they were elegant. Horses were kind and sensitive to each other's feelings. They took their time doing everything. The stallions loved noticing the mares and the mares loved watching the stallions show off for them. That was all too much 'nice' for Gwendolyn. She couldn't feign that kind of grace for long. And she didn't even want to try.

For the time being, frustrated Gwendolyn got into the routine of being a pretty cool cat. She ate. She groomed. She ignored them when they ignored her. She patrolled her regular stalking path around the farm. And she slept at night and put on makeup every morning.

From time to time, Gwendolyn would sneak over to the pigpen, and, without makeup, she would frolic as a pig would. Because now, time had passed, and she was no longer a piglet. She was a fully grown sow, a very pretty, fully grown sow.

One morning she woke up and realized in a panic that she had only enough makeup left to highlight how pretty of a sow she was. Without more makeup, she wouldn't be able to be a cool cat or anything else, including a pretty sow. And the only place she knew to go for more makeup was back at her home in the pigpen, from her mom, who had always bought Gwendolyn's makeup for her.

It was late in the morning, long after Rooster had crowed, and Gwendolyn knew she would have to be more careful than she had ever been before, if she wanted to get back into the pigpen without being noticed. She put on the rest of her makeup, highlighting her already pretty, pig face, and she began to make her way back home.

She was just entering the pen when she heard a vaguely familiar grunt.

“Hello,” said the deep voice that followed the grunt.

Gwendolyn turned around. She was looking directly into the face of a large boar smiling at her. He wasn’t wearing makeup, but he was wearing thick glasses, and his brown hair was parted to one side. She found him to be handsome.

“I’ve known you for a long time, Gwendolyn,” said the boar. “The first time I saw you was over by that water barrel. You were with your litter, and I was with mine. I thought you were such a pretty piglet.”

She didn’t remember him, but she smiled and pretended she did. She looked perfect to him, and her smile convinced him that she did remember him.

“Are you going to stay this time?”

Gwendolyn was startled and didn’t know how to answer his question.

“This time,” he repeated. “Are you going to stay? I’ve seen you here at night. Now and then you show up. For a while I didn’t know who you were until one night the moon was full and I could see your face. And it was you, Gwendolyn. Every time I watched you rolling in the mud and slopping from the trough, all I could think of was how much I wanted a pretty sow just like you to spend the rest of my days with.”

And that’s when she remembered that this boar had been one of the piglets she had liked talking to when they were very small.

“Arthur!” she said, hugging him tightly. “I have thought

about my old friend every day, wondering how you are." She hadn't really wondered how he had been but Arthur was easily convinced. Gwendolyn was smiling.

"You were always my best friend. You listened to my ramblings, and you always understood me."

Arthur was dizzy.

Gwendolyn and Arthur spent the entire day talking and catching up. She told him that she had gone away looking for someone who could understand her and love her. She meant it. She only returned to the pigpen in secret because she had always felt drawn to come back, for a reason that was unknown to her, she told him. She also told him that it was probably the universe leading her back and wanting them to connect, and therefore she and Arthur were meant to connect. Gwendolyn didn't mean it but she looked like she did.

"I understand you!" Arthur meant it, although he didn't know it wasn't true. "I watched you every night you climbed back into the pigpen. You were the prettiest piglet I'd ever seen. And I followed you into the woods, by moonlight, when you rooted for truffles that you ate by yourself. I understand you, Gwendolyn. You love being a pig more than anything else. And I love you more than anything else."

Deep inside, Gwendolyn was embarrassed and a little upset that Arthur had been watching her. She didn't like sharing her secrets with anyone. But she couldn't help loving Arthur's compliments. He paid them to her frequently and each one was unique.

Gwendolyn had only ever intended on sticking around the

pigpen until her mom bought her more makeup. But after spending a few days with Arthur and his constant attention and adoration for her, she started to devise a new plan. And when Arthur told her how much all of the other boars envied him and wished they were Arthur who's sow was the prettiest pig on the farm, Gwendolyn knew exactly what she wanted to be, finally.

A few weeks later Gwendolyn and Arthur were married. Gwendolyn never looked prettier and happier marrying Arthur. Her makeup was flawless. The wedding was the finest ever attended on that farm and everyone had a wonderful time celebrating what was the ideal union, a respectable boar, and the prettiest sow.

Arthur and Gwendolyn led very comfortable lives after that. They were well liked and admired in the community. Arthur spent lots of time with the other boars when he wasn't telling his wife how beautiful she was.

Gwendolyn was adored every day by Arthur, who also gladly gave her lots of money so she could buy lots of makeup. And she received praise wherever she went, all around the farm.

"Gwendolyn, you are the prettiest pig anyone has ever seen. Your mom must be so proud."

That was the polite way of saying that she was prettier than her mom, Gwendolyn thought.

And though they never had their own litter, Arthur and Gwendolyn never wanted for anything on that pretty farm by the pretty stream that ran down into that pretty valley surrounded by those pretty mountains.

Every so often though, when Arthur is fast asleep and snoring, Gwendolyn quietly puts on fresh makeup and she heads out far beyond the confines of the farm, to distant parts with new animals who haven't yet seen how pretty Gwendolyn is.

Fin de la Fin

"You're here!"

"Absolutely."

He stood up to greet his friend. They used to meet every morning. For years they did. And then it was once a week. Now they meet once a month, more or less, in the diner they had been coming to for years, and it hadn't really changed.

"I didn't think they were going to let you out," he said with a big grin.

"Well you know, now and then I gotta get the stink blowed off of me, as they say." His friend exaggerated a made up Southern drawl. "I'm surprised they let you in."

The banter could have gone on and they both knew it. They watched their waitress pour coffee. She was friendly, nice looking. She was new to them.

The men took their time preparing their cups of fresh coffee. He only liked cream, just a little. His friend liked his coffee black.

They sipped the steaming coffee without saying much of anything or feeling like they needed to for a spell.

"So, what's new? Do you have anything good?" He watched his friend grimace and struggle for a comfortable position in the booth before answering.

"Well, Sir, I'll tell you what's good is that there's nothing bad to tell."

He smiled at his friend. "Not bad is pretty good."

“I don’t suppose I hear from anyone we know,” his friend thought.

“I’m not sure there is anyone we know,” he said quickly.

The two friends laughed together and for a minute that is all that there was.

“I've been working on it again, the script...you know that I know this story inside and out." He took a sip.

"I do know."

"I'm working on it all the time now...'course not when I had the flu."

"No kidding? That leveled me good. A month. A month!"

"Uh, Huh. It was bad this year."

They both stopped talking and drank their coffees.

"I do like that story though. It's a good one. I liked it the first time you told it to me. After you thought it up. When was that? College?"

His friend nodded. "I didn't know what I was talking about back then." He was again adjusting to the booth. His body seemed to creak. “It was before all that other stuff.”

He ignored his friend’s last comment. "It was a great story. It still is. It’s a helluva movie."

"I'm giving myself a deadline this year. June 15. It was my old man's birthday."

"Yeah?"

They sort of smiled and sort of nodded in agreement.

"I think about that old man. All the time. I do," his friend said.

“He was a good man.” He had always replied this way and he didn’t know why. But he did know what his friend always said back and why he said it.

“I wish,” his friend said.

The waitress set out menus and silverware. The two men picked up the menus and perusing them, they discussed economics, politics, and their declining financial situations, without saying a word. When the conversation was over—a system of sighs, grumbles, and head nods and shakes—they both ordered the same things they had always ordered.

"Do you still think about it?"

"Sometimes I don't. But usually I'm reminded about it every day at least once."

"It shouldn't have happened."

"It happened."

"It shouldn't have."

"It did."

“Still…”

This topic of conversation hardly went beyond a few lines. It had run its course years ago and only habit brought it up when they had breakfast. The routine exchange was always quick and it always left hard space.

Their attention was easily drawn to the young family that was just being seated at a table near theirs. The couple were in their twenties, probably. The pretty mom helped her daughter up into the chair next to her while the smart looking husband helped the son. The daughter could have been three and the son five. But the two men didn't think about it too much. The father took the mothers hand and held it tightly, in the open, on the table. They were all smiling.

The two men noticed each other watching the family. The man knew that his friend was thinking about children. The friend knew that the man was thinking about a wife and holding hands. But these were things that they no longer needed to talk about. They had been friends the whole time, along the whole journey, and they had seen everything each other had seen. And they had seen them in the same way. Secretly though, they both knew the reason they didn't talk about it anymore was because it no longer mattered. When the advice turned into self-deprecating humor that turned into melancholy and regret, they had stopped talking about things. And now things were far in the past.

They ate their breakfasts and pretended not to notice that each was eating just a little slower and with greater pauses between bites. They were messier eaters now, too.

When they finished eating, the waitress walked over and cleared away their plates, wiped their table and poured fresh coffee. The men only glanced at the young family, cheerfully eating their breakfasts -- husband and wife quietly talking, and their children, whose legs were swinging to and fro under the table.

Three men sitting over at the counter were suddenly energized and loud. They were recalling highlights from a game long since played. They were arguing about the outcome, the drive, the missed last second field goal, and which team had actually been better that year.

The two friends smiled when their waitress, filling the three men's coffees, chimed in about the game with a remark that left everyone at the counter laughing loudly before things returned to normal.

The two friends shook their heads, chuckled a little, and sipped their coffees.

"Whatever happened to that kicker?"

"Not sure. He was good though. Really good."

"One missed kick."

"Yep."

"One missed kick. An entire season and one missed kick."

"Yep."

The two friends sipped coffee and didn't speak again until the waitress brought the check. They left cash on the table and they agreed to meet again for breakfast soon.

Outside the diner they laughed over familiar jokes and they waited until their rides picked them up and drove them away, one and then the other, ten minutes apart.

On Harry's Birthday

By the time Harry was dyed, they'd been doing it so long few folks remembered that it had once been a law. They'd dye you at five and before that only your parents and doctor would see you. And you never went out. Harry was dyed on his fifth birthday.

"Why am I getting dyed?" Harry asked.

"Because everyone does, Son."

"Why does everyone get dyed?" Harry asked.

"So everyone has the same skin, Son."

Harry thought. He put his right hand up to his chin and wrinkled his brow. He was a very bright five-year-old.

"Is skin important?"

"It can be."

Harry looked at his forearms and his smooth, newly dyed skin.

"Did you love me yesterday?"

"Of course we did," they both said.

"We always love you," his mother assured him, kissing his cheek, still warm from the dying.

After Harry was dressed a woman opened the door to lead

them out. She was the first new person he had ever seen. Harry thought she was beautiful.

There were more new people, men, and women, in the hallway. They were attractive too, Harry noticed. They smiled cheerfully at Harry and his parents when they passed by. More handsome new people helped them complete the data forms, lead them to the elevators, opened doors, and helped them out of the building and into his parents' steam sedan. A handsome man, older than Harry but younger than Harry's parents was holding the sedan door open for them. Harry saw he was dressed all in black.

"Jeffrey, meet Harry. Harry, this is Jeffrey." His father introduced them.

"Hello, Harry. I am very glad to meet you finally." Jeffrey smiled and shook Harry's hand. "You sure do have beautiful eyes, just like your father." Jeffrey smiled wider.

"Beautiful eyes like his mother," Harry's father corrected, and they both laughed.

His mother rolled her eyes.

Harry wanted to laugh too but didn't because he wasn't sure what the joke was. Maybe it's funny because he and his parents all had the same looking dark brown eyes.

After Jeffrey had helped them in and closed the door, he had gotten into the front seat and was now driving them through the city. In the backseat of the big sedan, Harry sat between his parents. This was his first time seeing his home city outside of pictures and videos. He had been brought to the clinic for his dying in a trunk carrier so no one would see him. When his father saw his son straining to see outside, he picked Jeffrey up and sat him next to the window. Harry was overwhelmed.

"It's a lot to take in all at once, isn't it, Harry? Believe you me, I still remember what it was like for me after I got dyed. I wanted to see everything." It was Jeffrey.

Harry could see the side of Jeffrey's face watching the road and calmly driving his family through the city. Seeing Jeffrey's reflection in the rear-view mirror, Harry liked Jeffrey's constant smile and the neatly trimmed mustache that made the smile seem bigger. Harry noticed Jeffrey's bright green eyes too and thought that Jeffrey had a friendly face.

In a short time, Jeffrey had turned the steamer down a long, curved drive. He stopped the steamer in front of a white marble building that was many stories high. People were waiting to help Harry and his parents. A woman helped them out of the car, and she wore red. She had brown hair and green eyes like Jeffrey's.

A man who ushered them through the gold front doors wore a grey jacket and thick black glasses that framed his blue eyes. Two teenagers who held the doors open wore gold jackets that matched the doors.

Harry watched a tall man in a blue suit walk right up to his father. He was smiling and Harry saw that his eyes were just like Harry's dad's and mom's, deep brown. The man shook his father's hand and hugged his mom and kissed her cheek. The man knelt in front of Harry.

"Happy Birthday, Harry! I am so glad to finally meet you. Your mom and dad and I have been friends since we were your age!"

Harry shook the man's hand.

"You can call me Uncle Owen, Harry."

The man turned to a pretty, young woman in a brown jacket. "Colin, please show our birthday guest of honor and his parents to his suite. I will be up in just a few minutes…Happy Birthday, Harry!"

"Yes, Sir," Colin smiled. She had long, blonde hair and blue eyes. Harry found Colin especially attractive.

Colin led the family up a wide staircase. She led them into an elevator and up to the seventh floor. The doors opened onto a log pier alongside a river that, flowing left to right, emerged from, and then disappeared into a thick jungle. Colin held the elevator doors open until a man wearing a safari outfit and carrying a torch walked over to them. He had dirty blonde hair that fell out from under a wide brimmed safari hat. He had a tan face and dull yellow eyes that nearly matched his canvas outfit.

"Happy Birthday, Harry!" he said.

Harry smiled, and the man helped them into a log canoe that had pulled up to the dock. Harry sat in the front of the boat. The man shoved them off and the canoe carrying the three slipped between flowering vines and the dock behind them disappeared.

"Remember Harry. Nothing in here can hurt you. These are projections, just like your games at home."

"OK," Harry said to his dad. He had already suspected as much.

The canoe picked up speed and the sound of approaching rapids grew louder. Harry saw a giant snake hanging from a tree as their canoe glided between two rocks and through the rapids. Harry was thrilled.

The river brought Harry past ancient ruins and sand shores lined with crocodiles; volcanoes erupting and pouring out lava; temples with smoke and chanting and the shadows of dancers; primitive villages both abandoned and alive and teaming with natives. Flocks of parrots filled the trees. There were flowers whose beauty was beyond description, wearing colors without names.

The ride was exhilarating, and Harry and his family were absolutely delighted when their canoe finally came to a stop at a dock made of logs. Uncle Owen was waiting for them.

"Wasn't that fun, Harry?" Uncle Owen bellowed.

Two men holding torches led the party of four from the dock and down a pathway lined with torches. The two men smiled at Harry, and he noticed how much their kind eyes reminded him of Jeffrey's.

The path led them to a large tent. Inside, the tent was lined with tables filled with endless varieties of food and drink. There were ice statues and chocolate fountains and in the center of the tent was a great champagne fountain shaped like the globe. And everywhere there were tables piled and overflowing with ornately wrapped gifts for Harry. The tent was crowded with people and Harry noticed that a great many of the guests appeared to be his age or, just a little older.

When Harry entered the tent everyone yelled, "Happy Birthday, Harry!" and they sang "Happy Birthday."

Harry could barely keep up with the rest of the evening. There were so many people to meet. His parents had many, many friends. The older kids thought it was cool that Harry was dyed on his birthday. By the end of the party, Harry was so exhausted, he could only nod his head when anyone talked to him.

Later that night after they had gotten home, Harry was lying in his bed, beneath thick, soft blankets, and remembering his big day. He remembered the warm feeling under his skin and all through his body when he was dyed. He remembered the different people in the dying center who were all so nice to him. He remembered Jeffrey's kind voice and bright green eyes. He remembered the comfortable seat in the back of the sedan and gazing through the wide window at that marvelous city, his city, alive with lights, and vehicles that flew around buildings that hovered and the endless variety of people moving about in an endless variety of speeds and directions, wearing an endless variety of colors, not unlike the flowers in the virtual jungle.

Harry thought about all the people at his party and the thought about all the gifts that he had received. All of the children and their parents were so friendly and so happy to meet him. A lot of the kids gave him envelopes full of money. But his two favorite gifts came from the two kids his age who he'd spent the most time with at the party and who became his buddies.

Daniel gave Harry a hovercar coupe and Meegin gave Harry a mini submarine that was just perfect for the huge lake south of the city.

"Think of all the adventures we can have now," Meegin had said excitedly more than a few times. Their faces had lighted up and Harry remembered wondering if his brown eyes sparkled like Daniel and Meegin's brown eyes did when they laughed. Daniel's parents and Meegin's parents had been friends since childhood with Harry's parents.

He was thinking about it all when his father came in to tuck him in for bed. Gerald, who worked for his parents in their home and whom Harry had only met when they came home that night, stood outside the door in a stiff tan jacket.

"It was quite a night, wasn't it, Son?" His father sat on the side of Harry's bed.

"There were lots of people."

Harry's father nodded.

"Everyone was nice to me."

"They are very nice people, Harry. They care about you."

Harry remembered the city and all the busy looking people.

"There are a lot of people in the city, aren't there, Dad?"

"There are."

"Are they all nice, too, Dad?"

"Pretty much, Son. They are."

"We all have the same skin."

"We do."

Harry remembered all of the different styles and colors of clothes and all the new people he had seen that day.

"Skin doesn't seem very important, Dad."

"You're right."

"Are people nice when they don't get dyed?"

"Not always, Son. That's why, a long time before you were born, Great-Great-Great Grandpa Emmitt helped create the dye. So people wouldn't be mean to each other because their skins were all different. Grandpa Emmitt didn't like to see folks being unkind."

"He was a nice man."

"He was a very nice man, Harry. He was a smart man and a successful man who made a lot of money. People liked him. He took care of his family. He made sure we could all live happy lives."

"Some kids gave me money for my birthday."

"That's a very nice gift."

"Do I need money, Dad?"

"No. Not really. But it is always nice to have, Harry." His father smiled.

"This week I'm going on an adventure in my submarine with Daniel and Meegin. They are my new friends."

"I'm glad they are, Harry. Your mother and I are very fond of their parents."

Harry reached for his dad who leaned close so Harry could hug his father's neck.

Harry's father kissed his cheek and told his son how proud of him he was. He got up from the side of the bed and left the bedroom. He turned to Gerald, still standing by the door.

"Gerald, please make sure Harry is comfortable before you turn out the light. After that you may go. You won't be needed again until morning."

Gerald nodded, and Harry's father turned and walked down the hall toward his study.

Harry watched Gerald come into his room, pick up Harry's dirty clothes from the floor and put them in the hamper. Gerald leaned over the bed and tucked Harry in tightly under the covers.

"Happy Birthday, Master Harry," Gerald said softly and smiled. "Sweet dreams."

Gerald's voice was smooth and kind. And his bright green eyes were just like Jeffrey's bright green eyes.

Gerald turned out the light and quietly closed the bedroom door.

Harry fell asleep thinking about how kind both Jeffrey and Gerald had been.

The Third Day

"My God..."

It was something he remembered, or thought he remembered. He mumbled it again without understanding. They were just words, sounds.

"Oh, God..."

The sweat poured. It felt heavy everywhere it ran down his skin. He tried to hold his eyes shut and found that he didn't have enough strength and the streams wound their way beneath his lids and burned. His vision was blurred by the pools sitting on his eyes.

"...why..."

He swallowed and it scratched his dry and thirsty throat. He decided he would not open his mouth again.

"...why...me." His lips barely moved.

Alone with his dying body, the struggle pushed him like water building up at the bow of a fishing boat in a strong current. It kept getting heavier and heavier and everything moved more and more slowly.

He remembered fishing on the big lake once, when a storm came on fast. Everyone else had been scared. He remembered being calm when the water piled up at the front of the boat and the boat struggled and stretched for the safety of shore. Everyone on board had looked to him for comfort.

His father had never taken him fishing. His father didn't fish.

For a moment he forgot the stinging eyes and dry throat. His father hadn't really taken him anywhere. He searched for his father in every memory he could recall, but he just wasn't there.

"Where was he?"

His heart pounded, pushing what felt like hot oil through his veins, burning his skin from the inside, and boiling the sweat that covered him like gasoline. He felt himself passing out and going someplace else, someplace he had forgotten.

"You're funny," he heard her say. Her voice was faraway.

She was driving and he was looking at her from the passenger seat. She glanced over to see him looking at her and quickly looked back at the road.

"We were driving past the old mission and you said we should call a realtor to look at that house. You said how much you liked the yard. You called it our 'dream home'."

She was referring to the 18th century, stone, Catholic mission. They had driven by the vast garden that highlighted the front of the mission grounds on their way home from the surgery center. Endless varieties of spring roses exploded with color.

"Good morning! We will be home in a minute." She smiled but didn't turn her head.

He didn't smile. He was still waking up. The surgery had been that morning and he was coming down from the anesthetic. He was groggy piecing things together as she drove them home. Seeing the cast on his left arm brought it back.

She parked the car in the driveway, made sure she had her cup of coffee and purse, and went to unlock the front door. He was slow and staggered a bit, walking himself from the car to the apartment they lived in. She looked awkward watching him walk, he noticed, as if she couldn't decide, or wasn't sure, if she should help him. She pushed the front door open and got out of his way.

He made it inside. He helped himself to the bathroom to urinate. When he finished, he made his way to the living room where he sat and rested the casted left arm on the back of the couch.

Her fingers were clasped together tightly. She was fidgeting. She was uncomfortable and was readying herself to leave. He was watching her.

"I bought you juice. Do you want me to put it in the refrigerator for you so it will get cold?" she asked.

"No. It's ok. I can use ice. I'll be ok."

"Are you sure?"

"Yes. I'd rather have ice. It's perfect." He was still groggy and slurred his words slightly.

She smiled. Nervously she excused herself to go back to work and then the door shut, the car backed out the drive, and he was there sitting on the couch, quietly feeling himself return to normal, except for his tightly bandaged, very numb left arm.

He sat for a minute. She had actually gone to the store and gotten him that juice that he liked so very much. She had never done that before when he had two arms, and he thought it made him feel good inside that she did. It had only taken surgery, he joked. He didn't think his joke was funny.

He stood cautiously and went to the kitchen to pour himself a glass of the juice. He found a glass, filled it with ice, and then opened up the cloth grocery bag with the juice in it. He pulled the plastic bottle out and placed it on the counter next to the glass.

He stopped. These were all things he could do with one arm.

He laughed.

He remembered the Twilight Zone episode about the thickly spectacled man who, alone in a post-apocalyptic world void of people, discovers he has nothing but time to read all of the books in the world. It is at that very moment that the man drops and breaks his only pair of glasses.

"She didn't think about it. I can only use one arm. I can't open the bottle." It would take two hands to twist the bottle to create the torque that would break the plastic seal and open the cap. This was funny.

Ignoring the juice glass, he filled another glass with tap water. He didn't use any ice. The warm tap water felt course in his mouth. It wasn't ice cold juice and it didn't make him feel better inside and the memory was over.

"Forsaken." He heard himself mumbling.

He was becoming conscious again and he felt the salty water bubbling on his lips. He knew he was fading in and out of his life. It made him profoundly sad, this story about juice.

"Forsaken."

He hadn't seen his ex-wife in eighteen years, which was also as long as they had been married. He thought back but he had so little strength.

Eighteen years should have filled his mind with memories of his life with her. But they didn't. 'Eighteen' was no magic number, no angel number, where they were concerned. Their pact had created nothing, produced nothing, and provided neither comfort nor grace, then or now. When he tried to drift back to it, there was nowhere to go. There was no light and no new perspective that could provide new insights. There was nothing of value to be gleaned. There had only been her and those empty years with her. He pushed away the memory of her and those nervous and fidgeting fingers for the last time.

He searched in vain for any memory of a warm hand against his cheek or a soft kiss on his forehead. They simply didn't exist and he knew that they didn't exist. There had never been anyone and shortly there never would be. He couldn't believe it. He had spent his entire life confiding in a God that wouldn't let that happen to him or anyone.

Everything was getting heavier, like all of gravity had discovered him, and time was slowing down. It was a struggle to reason and to hope and to pray. It was a struggle to ignore the very essence of his soul demanding to know why, at the end of his life, he still had to hope and pray, like the punchline to a knock-knock joke that is self-perpetuating. It is a cruel joke that begins with every possibility and goes nowhere.

Even now with so few breaths left to breathe, he needed to believe in the impossible. He needed to believe that the prayer that he kept with him each day of his life, a short prayer asking only to find love, would finally be answered. He needed to know that the silence he was reaching out to during all of those moments in what felt like a very empty life, wasn't really silent. Wouldn't that finally make everything that had come before worthwhile, even with so little time now?

"Come...please...please…create" He didn't understand what he was muttering before he was unconscious again.

The House Across the Road

Kenneth and his grandfather watched from the front porch as the ambulance screamed its way through the neighborhood and backed into the driveway of the house across the road, where the woman lived. EMTs rushed, pushing a metal stretcher that reflected the sun's sharp rays and looked heavy.

Earlier that afternoon, just before Kenneth called 911, he and his grandfather were enjoying the warm spring day and sipping sweet tea. They watched the woman's oldest daughter park in front of the house and go inside carrying groceries for her mother, as she frequently did. After the screen door closed with a snap behind her, they heard her crying out.

Mama?

Mama, please, I need you to wake up!

Please, Mama. Wake up!

Please wake up!

Kenneth and his grandfather had passed years sitting together on that screened-in porch, since the roads were dusty, red clay, and you could still see the lagoon across the road. Decades earlier, when Kenneth was nine, he was still Kenny then, he went to live with his grandparents. His parents had decided to stop pretending that they loved each other and divorced. Shortly thereafter, on his ninth birthday, Kenny's mom decided to stop pretending she liked being a mom and she left him with her parents. She had also decided she did not like being a daughter anymore and so Mimi and Pa and Kenny would never hear from her again.

Mimi and Pa, were loving people, and Kenny liked growing up in their house. Mimi shared her love for books and Kenny became a voracious reader. But more than anything Kenny loved sitting on the screened-in porch with Pa. In all but the worst weather, they watched the seasons turning and the neighborhood changing. And the porch was their island of two where the screens kept the passing of time at bay.

After dinner and on weekends they retreated to that screened-in porch. Sitting on wooden chairs with soft cushions that Mimi had made, Pa and Kenny took in ball games, the world news, and the Prairie Home Companion, on a dime store FM radio. And when they weren't listening to the radio, they were talking. Pa was a thoughtful and insightful man with a sense of humor, and he shared his love for conversation with his grandson. Pa never talked down to Kenny, as if he were a child. It felt good spending time with Pa because Pa made everyone feel important and Kenny cherished it.

One summer the county paved the road. It was hard work in a hot Florida sun. The sweat poured and the new asphalt reeked. He and Pa stayed on the porch, cooled only by the shade and an old metal fan that squeaked out an odd rhythm. They listened to the Braves on the radio, drank sweet tea, and watched workers pave the road. On their last day of work, Kenny helped Pa give them each a beer.

Two falls later they watched as their view of the lagoon disappeared when a house went up. The house did not look like much. It was a plain rectangular blue box on stilts with windows. Its roof was a triangle. A single window on either side of the front door, along with the steps leading up to the front door and surrounding deck, created a face that made the house seem as if it might just get up on those stilts and walk, or jump away, like a witch's house.

Kenny turned twelve when she moved in. He had finished riding the bike he had gotten for his birthday, and he was sitting on the porch with Pa when she pulled into the driveway and stepped out of a red, convertible Mustang. In the passenger seat Century 21 realtor's Open House signs with her picture on them were tangled in a bunch. She did not look like a witch. A young forty-looking, she was medium height. She had big blue eyes that could be seen from across the road when she took off her sunglasses. She had long, soft wavy brown hair. Her big smile revealed even white teeth and deep dimples on her cheeks. When she waved and said, "Hey, Sweetie," she had a soulful southern drawl that made Pa blush.

Kenny and his grandfather would come to know this woman, but only as neighbors get to know each other, at the end of the driveway or in the middle of the road, on the friendliest of terms, and without ever truly getting to know each other. Her name was Sarah.

Sarah was separated from her husband, she said, though she used the words *separated* and *divorced* interchangeably. It would be several years before she would stop using the word *separated* altogether. She was a real estate agent. She had two daughters that lived with their father and occasionally stayed with their mother. In time, the younger daughter would stop visiting entirely.

For years, even after the actual divorce, Sarah's ex-husband would stop by, usually to pressure wash, or paint the house, or mend a front step. On occasion he would use his truck to help her move a new piece of furniture in or an old one out. Every so often he would spend the night. But at some point, he too stopped coming by.

Sitting on the porch, it did not take long before Kenny and Pa knew something certain about the house across the road. It was her secret to all but a few people in her life. And when those people stopped being a part of Sarah's life, her secret grew smaller.

Just after Sarah moved in, there was a boyfriend. He was tan and tall. His hair was blonde from dye and expensively styled and he constantly wore a half-smile that was friendly but not kind. His white BMW, license plate *1RLTR1,* often spent nights parked in her driveway, especially over the first three years that Sarah lived there. And then for a while his Beemer was not there nearly as often. And then it was not there for a long time, for more than a year. And then, briefly, they saw the Beemer parked there every day. And then Kenny and Pa never saw it again.

On nights the BMW was not there and throughout the years, Kenny and his grandfather had seen more than a few cars spending the night parked in the driveway across the road. Most belonged to men but some belonged to women. Every so often a car would return for a night or two, or a week, or maybe for a month. Most cars were not seen again in that driveway. But there were a few of the cars that they did get to know.

There was the maroon 1967 Plymouth Barracuda that, for a few years, seemed to stop by like clockwork every three months. He always wore a dark blue suit, light blue shirt untucked, and no tie. He would knock on the door. They would go for a ride, and he would stay for the night. Kenny and his grandfather loved that Barracuda, and they missed it when it was gone.

The Christmas she moved in, Sarah decorated her house with lights and angels and a nativity scene. She also decorated for Easter and Halloween that year and this became a tradition that the neighborhood anticipated as her decorations were so elaborate. And then one Christmas she did not decorate and never decorated again. It stopped around the same time that the Beemer left for good, and when Kenny was in high school.

For a long time after that Christmas, until he finished high school, Kenny did not see Sarah, just her car when it was parked in the driveway, and the lights when they were on inside her house. And then he went away to college.

Kenny spent his first summer break back home doing restaurant work. He worked late nights, until long after his grandparents had gone to bed. He did not have a social life and he did not mind. College had been fun. He was looking forward to getting back in the fall with money to spend. Each night, after work, Kenny showered and put on running shorts – the summer nights were too muggy for a shirt. He relaxed on the porch, listening to the radio, getting stoned, and smoking a cigarette or two before going off to bed.

On the night of the Fourth of July, Kenny had worked later than usual because of the tourists and the holiday crowd flocking to the beaches. It was just around one in the morning when he sat down on the porch. He tipped his head back and let it rest against Mimi's soft cushion sticking up from the back of the chair. It had become perfectly fitted to his head over the years and it felt good. He closed his eyes, and he kept them closed when he heard her car speeding around the corner and up the road. He opened them after she swerved into her driveway, braked, and killed the engine all at once.

For several minutes Kenny watched Sarah sitting in the dark. When she opened the car door, he could see that she was wiping her face with her left hand, like wiping away tears, he thought. She got out of the car and closed the door. She was standing and looking in Kenny's direction. The moon was bright, making Kenny visible as a dark form holding the red glow from the tip of the joint he was smoking. With her hands, she smoothed her short black dress that reflected bits of the moonlight when it moved.

"Do you have a cigarette?"

He thought he heard her correctly, but he was not sure. He did not want her to have to raise her voice this late at night and so he left the porch and walked quickly over to her. Watching him walk to her, she smiled, looking nothing at all like someone who might have been crying just minutes before.

"Do you have a cigarette, Kenny?" Sarah smelled good to him; her perfume was sweet. He might have noticed a hint of alcohol.

"I do."

She watched him open his pack and start to pull out the last cigarette to give to her. She stopped him by putting her right hand on top of his.

"I'm not going to take your last cigarette, Sweetie." She did not slur her words.

"No. It's OK. I am going to get a fresh pack in the morning. Besides, I have a joint in the ashtray on the porch. Please, take it."

She smiled and lit the cigarette with a lighter from her purse. "When I moved here, I was taller than you. You're tall, Kenny.

And now you've already graduated high school."

"Yes, Ma'am. I'm in college now. I'm just home for the summer."

She took a long drag. She was smiling widely when she exhaled a thick cloud of white smoke.

"No more, Ma'am, OK, Kenny? In fact, no more Kenny.

You're too tall for Kenny. Besides, you're a college man now. You're a Kenneth…Go get your joint, Kenneth. Let's smoke it inside."

Kenneth almost said 'yes, Ma'am' but he caught himself and grinned. He ran over and grabbed his joint and ran back. He followed Sarah up the front steps. She opened the door, and he walked in behind her. It was his first time inside the house that he and his grandfather had watched being built. She gave him a quick tour without pausing too long in any one room.

Sarah's house was very clean, and it smelled like peaches, the way she smelled. Each room had its own color theme. It reminded him of an ad for a home décor store. There were fake flowers and plastic fruit arrangements in every room and the small dining room was set and ready for an intimate party of four. On the walls ornately framed commercial prints depicted imagined scenes of Paris and Parisian café life in a style that was pleasing and also not quite art.

Throughout the house there were framed wall hangings bearing inspirational sayings. Some were vaguely Christian – *God's Love Begins With You;* and others shared affirmations like

– *YOU are the SUNSHINE in EVERY DAY,* and *All You Are Is LOVE.* Kenneth noticed that with the exception of a couple of pictures of her daughters, and a picture of her holding up a glass of red wine overlooking a French vineyard, there were no personal photographs, and no photographs of men. Inside it looked happy, but somehow, it did not feel happy.

Sarah had, however, made a point of showing Kenneth a wrinkled black and white photo of her mother in a yellowed metal frame on the stand next to her bed. "That's my mama. Isn't she pretty?" she said.

Her bedroom had French doors leading on to an enclosed porch overlooking the lagoon. It was air conditioned. The view was, despite new houses on the opposite shore, still very pretty and, as Kenneth had remembered it. Sarah disappeared and came back moments later. She laid a fresh hard pack of cigarettes on the coffee table in front of the futon they were sitting on. She was still wearing the black dress with silver glitter that she had been wearing when she got home. Kenneth noticed how petit the dress was when she leaned over to hand him a beer.

"Here you go, college man."

Kenny thought she was teasing him innocently until she sat very close, with her hand on his bare shoulder.

It was past 4am when he got up to leave. Sarah was asleep on the futon. He walked past the kitchen. He saw her panties and bra on the floor by the refrigerator from when she had first gotten their beers. He closed the front door quietly behind him and he went across the road to sleep in his bed until it was time for him to get ready for work.

Late that night, when he got home from work, Sarah's car was not in the driveway. And she did not come home before Kenneth finally turned off the radio and went to bed. It was not there the next morning. And her driveway stayed empty for more than a week. On a Saturday morning Pa and Kenny went out on the porch with their coffees and her car was parked in her driveway. Kenneth spent a good part of his day watching the front door of the house across the road with expectations.

Late that afternoon, just before sunset, they saw her walking quickly to her car, as if she were late for an appointment. She saw the two men, waved, and sent them a saccharine, "Hey, Sweeties!" She did not wait to hear Kenneth, or his grandfather return the greeting. She got into her car and drove off into the evening. She was wearing the same black dress Kenny had known. It was as if nothing had happened between them. And that is how she acted when she politely smiled and waved the few times she saw him in the weeks before he went back to school.

This time when Kenneth left for college, he stayed gone for a long time. He earned his degree, taught high school for a couple of years, and then he went to graduate school. And for a time, he only came home to be with Mimi and Pa for holidays and over the winter breaks.

The Christmas before he finished his dissertation, he and his grandfather were drinking coffee on the porch. It was Christmas Eve morning. Kenneth was surprised when Sarah opened her front door, sat down in a chair next to it, lit a cigarette and smoked it fast. She lit a second cigarette off of the end of the first one. She smoked it quickly also, and then she went inside, slamming the door hard behind her.

Sipping their coffees, Pa and Kenneth watched Sarah. Neither of them said a word. Kenneth had not seen her in a very long time and the person he watched sit hunched over and smoking those cigarettes he did not recognize at all. And even after he did see that it was Sarah beneath that strange face, he had to keep reminding himself.

She was gaunt. Her skin, no longer tan, was pasty grey, spotted, and hung loosely. The lines on her face from years of smoking were deep furrows. Her blue eyes were dull, with barely a spark inside of them. Her dark hair was oily and stringy, and hung straight down from her head, like it had weight that caused her shoulders to sink. She was wearing a faded pink house coat and silver glittered house slippers.

He looked at his grandfather who knew what Kenneth was thinking.

"After a while the only one ever to stop by is her oldest daughter, taking care of her ma and bringing groceries, running errands."

Pa emptied his mug.

"Once in a while a friend from out of town stops by. But the only time I see her anymore is when she goes off to work or runs to the store for cigarettes and a box of that wine she drinks. I don't think we've said hello to each other in five years."
His grandfather was looking across the road. "Ignore it or not. That's just how it is."

The following year Kenneth was filling up his car to take his grandparents and his new fiancé out for dinner to celebrate Christmas Eve. Pumping the gas, he saw Sarah through the window of the Tom Thumb running the register. Interacting with the customers, her face was stern and stiff. She looked mean. He pretended not to notice her.

A couple of years later, Kenneth and his wife both got new university teaching positions. Before moving across the country, they spent spring and summer with Mimi and Pa. Kenneth's wife adored them like her own and Mimi loved having another woman in the house.

It had been a long time since that Fourth of July night and Kenneth had nearly forgotten it had ever happened. Over the years following, he had grown indifferent to the house across the road and any cars that might be parked in the driveway, including her car. In every respect she was simply the woman who lived in the house across the road and who used to, for a time when he was a boy, decorate the outside of her house brilliantly for the holidays. It was nostalgia as much as anything that kept Kenny looking across the road.

One afternoon a couple of days after Easter Sunday, Kenny and Pa were out on the porch listening to a baseball game when an ambulance pulled into the driveway across the road.

The ambulance had not been racing and its siren and lights had not been on. Medics went inside and carried her out on a stretcher and drove her away. Three weeks later, her oldest daughter brought her home from the hospital and helped her out of the car and up the front steps. Sarah was dragging her right leg. It seemed to hang from her side and dangle. Sarah's daughter held her tightly all the way up the steps and through the front door.

After that, her daughter, rarely accompanied by her husband who waited in the car when he did accompany her, stopped by regularly, usually to bring groceries and cigarettes and boxes of wine. Sometimes when she was alone Kenneth heard cursing, or a dish breaking, or yelling, coming from inside the house.

Very late one night, Sarah's granddaughter, with her boyfriend in tow, stopped by and there was arguing that went on between three loud voices. They started at the front door before eventually taking the argument inside. Other neighbors were disturbed by the yelling and a sheriff's car drove slowly by without stopping. That had been a year ago, and Kenneth had not seen the two again until today, when they had parked exactly where the funeral home van had been, before it left with her grandmother zipped in a dark plastic bag.

Kenneth and his wife were visiting Mimi and Pa for Easter. The ball game had been on, but Pa had turned the volume way down when Kenneth called 911, and then he turned the radio completely off out of respect for Sarah. Sitting on the porch Kenneth and Pa did not say much and simply watched the ambulance and the funeral home's van complete their business and drive away.

When Easter dinner was ready, Mimi came out to the porch. She had been cooking with Kenneth's wife all afternoon. She was still wiping her hands with a hand towel when she told them dinner was ready. And then her face turned dour, almost sad, as she looked at the dark, empty house. Kenneth could not remember ever hearing his grandmother mention Sarah or the house before.

"I went to school with Sarah's mama," Mimi said. "Starting in the second grade when she moved here from Tennessee. We were friends in middle school and her name was Grace. But Grace got mad at me for something I can't even remember. In high school Grace did what she wanted and came and went as she wanted. She was a pretty girl, so she got away with it. Grace dated who she wanted to date too.

I'm not sure she even thought about it much. Her daddy had money and she was used to getting things she wanted. Then I went off to college and came back and married your Pa.

"Grace was just out of high school when she had that baby girl. And we all knew the daddy. He sold yachts down at the marina. He had a lot of money, and he was twenty years older than Grace. He was also a mean drunk, who knocked the pretty out of her. I can't imagine being a little girl and growing up in a house like that. I can't imagine Grace would have done much to look out for her daughter. I can't imagine."

Mimi paused briefly.

"Your Pa and I saw Grace at a bar one night. She was wearing clothes that were too young and dancing with men who were too young. She wasn't there with her husband. Maybe he was at home. Sarah would have just been a teenager then."

Mimi looked across the road at the empty house. She mumbled, but Kenneth heard what she said.
"With her own hands, the foolish one tears hers down."
Mimi turned and the screen door closed quietly behind her. Pa and then Kenneth followed her inside to the dining room where Kenneth's wife was just lighting the candles for Easter dinner.

It's a Small Space

These days he stared at the blank screen.

Once, the computer had been central to his morning routine. Once, he would wake, drink coffee, briefly catch up on the news of the world, and then vigorously dive into his work. In those days, when his fingers reached out to the four corners of the globe, when they brought back those experiences and shaped them with words, he hated going to bed at night, and he couldn't wait to wake up each morning. He had done good work and it had been valued by people who loved him.

Today it was all he could do to drop his stiff, bent fingers onto the keyboard. He had insisted on bringing his old keyboard with him to this new place. The old keyboard had thick plastic keys that once echoed with a loudness that was both mechanical and organic. He pushed 'enter' on this computer and it whirred.

Outside, in the hall, he could hear the staff changing shifts. Muffled conversations and rolling carts were central to their morning routine. He smelled breakfast coming down from the dining room, scrambled eggs and coffee. It mixed with the ever-present smell of medicines and floor cleaner.

He sat perfectly still while the web site loaded. It didn't take long to open but he pretended it did. Sometimes, though, he wasn't sure if he was pretending. No matter. And today he didn’t feel like arguing with himself about it.

The computer stopped whirring. The web site opened but he didn’t see it.

Sitting there waiting, his eyes had closed and he could feel his lungs breathing in and out slowly. He drifts back to a long-forgotten sofa, where he is napping during a late afternoon rain, in front of a TV movie. Through drowsy eyelids he peeks at the black and white movie. It is about him.

It is an old movie, and in the movie, he finds himself in the back of a computer store. He is just a boy. Maybe nine. Maybe ten. Standing alone, he is transfixed by the new computers lined up along two aisles like titanium and black sports cars. Each monitor is cycling spectacular images of men exploring space, vast coral reefs, mountain tops encircled with clouds, and ancient ruins in dense jungles. He sees markets from faraway lands, exotic and bustling with people and animals. He sees aluminum jets and space craft streaking toward the heavens, scientists in laboratories working on robots, and Einstein.

The crispness of the never-before-seen images is intoxicating and their beckoning gnaws at his young insides. He wants one.

The computer clicks. It is a rude interruption and he is back in his room with the coffee and eggs smell. He ignores the impulse to open his eyes. He wants to see the movie play out.

Again, he is all the way in the back of the store, standing by the display, and now his father is there with him. The boy wants to ask his dad for the computer. He wants to show his dad all the things that he imagines doing with the computer. Things he'd share and that would make his father proud. He wants to show his dad that his brain is full of ideas and that he thinks about so many different things and it is because of his dad that he does. He wants his dad to know and to see his boy and to buy the computer.

But his father already has in hand what he had come to the store to purchase. And the father is ready to leave. And for his father, that is all that is important. The two walk quickly out of the store through sliding doors without a word ever being spoken about computers. The movie is over and the memory dissolves. And just as memories do, they leave an emptiness.

"A long time ago," the old man hears himself whisper.

Slowly blinking the light back into his eyes, the old man begins scrolling through the website that had been open now for some time.

Once, the news had documented a vastly more ambitious world than the one that presented itself to him anymore. Now it was all gossip about people he didn't recognize with names he unknowingly mispronounced. And the weather. He didn't have much use for any of it.

He looks around his room.

"It's a small space," he notes.

He shuts the computer down and watches as the screen empties and darkens. He pushes his chair away from the desk so the metal legs loudly scratch the tiled floor. He sits for a minute and then he stands, steadies himself, and pushes the chair noisily back under the desk.

Outside it looks to be a fine spring day. The metal blinds have cracks and light partially fills his room. A beam of sunlight flattens against the tightly shut door.

He wonders if it is cool outside. He opens his closet and, with no intention of going anywhere, he pretends to look for something warm to put on. He reaches for a wind breaker and it rustles the other hangers. The closet is mostly empty save for a couple of jackets, shirts, an old black suit, and the box.

He looks up at the box. The box is there on the high shelf, along with an electric blanket and an empty plastic container shaped like a barrel and which used to hold pretzels. The box is white, cardboard and plainly labeled with his last name, misspelled, across the side. He didn't like the error, even though it is a typo that ultimately will never amount to anything.

There had been plenty of times when he had reached for the box, taken it down, and confirmed that his items were still inside. And before that, there had been plenty of times when he made copies and shared things with other people who were interested in what he had done. And once there had been many other boxes full of many things and many people, interesting people, who valued those things, and learned from them. But now it is just the one box up on the thin wire frame shelf, typo and all. Forgetting the windbreaker, he closes the closet door.

He sits on the edge of his bed very still with his hands on his knees and stares out the window. His window faces a courtyard. The grass is green and freshly cut and stands out against the white stucco building. It makes the courtyard around the other wing look very clean.

A Sunday Visit

Claire was nervous and knowing she was going to arrive fifteen minutes late made her more so. He had said that he wanted her there at 2pm and while his tone was soft, it left her feeling that she must show up on time. Claire liked the sound of his voice and, it turned out, that that one phone call was not the first time she had heard him speak. It might turn out to be a fortuitous coincidence that her new online friend was a regular substitute teacher at the school where she worked, she mused. She remembered seeing him and saying 'hello' but she didn't remember liking his voice. That he did what she did and worked where she worked was comforting. And now she was late getting to his house.

Claire had been chatting with him for more than a week through the app on her phone. The app was designed to help folks find other folks with like interests. Adult interests. These interests, compiled and categorized by the creators of the app, could be checked off and posted prominently so as to attract like-minded new friends. This is where they met. Their purposefully shared interests, a couple of 'likes', and an introductory IM easily transformed into three or four days of very personal and intense messaging.

Before she knew it, Claire was sharing her entire life history with him. He sympathized with her. He offered insight and extended comfort when she described her mistakes and pains. He made her smile when the conversation became too dark. And he professed that the two shared a strong connection, a bond. He professed it to her a lot. It was obvious to her that he was trying not to be too obvious. But she didn't care. Claire liked the attention. And the conversations had depth. These were real conversations.

She shared her youthful explorations, a ravishing college affair, and the miserable marriages that left her feeling empty and lost. Claire delighted in describing her new life's aspirations as well as long held dreams she still cherished. And she shared with him experiences she found herself coveting more and more; experiences everyone around her was enjoying, everyone it seemed, but her. Mostly, she talked about her failed marriages and those lost years and what she would do if she could have them back. How much more living she would have done; how much more daring she would have been.

When Claire met her first husband he had swept her off of her feet with romance and attention. He gave her so much attention. It was her first relationship after college and it felt mature. He was in flight school for the Navy and she was going to be a Navy wife. Then, and she was never really sure exactly what happened, but something happened and he wasn't in the Navy anymore and then he was working as an insurance agent and making good money for the two of them to live very comfortable lives. Soon he stopped coming home at five and they stopped having dinners together and then breakfasts together and then the sex was gone and she found herself maintaining a very empty house with a man who was more like a brother than her husband, the Naval aviator she had fallen in love with.

After that divorce there was the teacher. He wasn't terribly romantic but he tried to sweep her off of her feet, as much as a high school math teacher was able. In other words, he was nice and he was stable. He liked her jokes. And he was always a gentleman with whom she felt safe. She entered this second marriage keeping a guarded distance though. And soon the intimacy, which hadn't really been all that intimate, was also gone. Her second marriage became a tight schedule that revolved around jobs and meals. Before long she was 38 years old and she couldn't remember the last time she had felt anything truly good or truly new.

Nine months after the second divorce was final Claire found herself, curiously, becoming curious. It was both strange and familiar. Along with staying up late for a movie on a school night, and rediscovering her passion for cooking, she was having sexual thoughts and a yearning for sexual experiences. This was the same yearning that found her when, at the age of ten, she stumbled upon her first centerfold. It was the first time she had seen a fully naked woman. She was posed erotically. Claire found herself excited and curious and full of so many needs, physical and otherwise she couldn't describe, because of the picture. Over time, marriage and life had buried this part of her. But Claire felt it returning and this reawakened need led her to install the app and create her profile. On only her second day, she connected with him and they began chatting.

Claire found it liberating to share so many intimate parts of her life with her new online friend. She discovered that these conversations, this virtual and living diary, became so much more. It satisfied so many aspects of who she was as an individual, aspects that had been long neglected. And now here, with him, texting felt like psychoanalysis. Or it felt like confession; or career counseling; or an art history seminar; or book club; or a letter to Santa Claus. The conversations seemed to float seamlessly from one topic to the next. Claire was getting out so many things that she hadn't really discussed with anyone. And she found she had been holding a lot inside.

Underpinning all of this, and in every respect giving shape and structure to these written conversations, was the fact that they were getting to know each other on a site where people meet specifically to hook up sexually. Whether it was prompted by the site or some truth about herself she was beginning to discover, most of their conversations segued into detailed written discussions about sex and sexuality, and she let them. With the illusion of distance, the two were able to discuss sex and obliquely flirt while they got to know each other. It made her feel young.

It surprised her when he told her about his past. She couldn't believe that a woman had treated this man, who seemed so thoughtful and so sweet, just as neglectfully as her men had treated her. His stories of being married and feeling alone were so familiar. She felt close to him, as if they had both been through the same war. When all at once he shared his identity and that he was that regular substitute teacher. His dramatic revelation was perfectly timed. It disarmed her. The conversation became sexually intimate.

After that, all of their conversations were sexual. The new online thrill was consuming and the next few days were dizzying, a passionate blur. And before she knew it, she had talked to him on the phone, and he had given her directions to his house, and had told her with his attractive sounding voice that 2pm on Sunday would be fine. And now it was Sunday and she was arriving late.

He was waiting for her on the porch.

"You wore the sundress. Good. But you are late."

Claire smiled naively.

"I'm sorry. I didn't realize I needed to stop and get gas."

He smiled at her and practically cut her off. "You are late."

He reached for her hand. Claire gave it to him and he led her into his living room. She barely had time to take in the room. She was still processing that this new physical person was her virtual online friend. She was waiting for him to start a conversation, as he had when they were texting.

"Let me take your purse."

Claire liked his voice in person.

She handed him her purse. He walked behind her and placed it on an end table beside the couch. She was taking in the living room in front of her. She recognized a 9th grade history textbook from her school near the computer desk in the corner.

Claire felt him standing behind her and somehow she knew she was not supposed to turn around. She wanted to but she stood still.

He whispered in her ear, "You were late. That is bad. But you wore the dress I asked you to wear. That is good."

Her eyes were wide. She didn't answer. Breaths from his whispers gave the back of her neck a chill.

Claire didn't move when he wrapped the silk scarf over her eyes and around her head until she couldn't see. Blind folded and standing still in the middle of the living room she could feel him looking at her. It was true, all the rest of her senses did come alive when her vision disappeared. She could feel him circling her, slowly. She could feel him looking at her. She liked the feeling.

And then in one motion he pulled the straps off of her shoulders. The dress fell to her feet. Again she was surprised that she didn’t resist. Standing before this new person that wasn't exactly a stranger, blindfolded, and in his living room, Claire was bare except for her panties. She hadn't worn a bra.

All of their conversations flooded her brain. They had been fueled by her curiosity, her need to know. She had encouraged him online. The excitement was building in her and she wanted to speak but her voice didn’t want to move. She wanted to celebrate her personal victory. She was taking control of her life.

He tied her wrists behind her back. He removed her panties. She was conscious of the fact that her panties were damp. She could tell that after he took them off of her, he held them briefly. She was a little embarrassed.

Though it was quiet, it was loud inside her head. She felt his hands moving over her. She liked being naked where he was still dressed. His hands felt new and soft and moved over her chest. She felt her body stiffen, responding to the touches. She felt her smooth back and curved hips when he moved his hands over her. She felt her muscled legs tighten, inside and out. And she felt the moisture when he cupped her. Goose bumps spread across her body and she heard herself sigh. It was relaxing.

“You were late.”

Reminding her, he led her by her tied wrists over to the couch and bent her over the arm. Leaving her like that he walked into the next room. She thought she heard his muffled voice talking with another muffled voice. And then it was quiet. And then he was back in the room.

He walked directly to her. She heard a plastic click and then felt his hand cold and wet hand touching her. Her husbands had never touched her there. She felt his finger pushing inside her. It reminded her of being young, before her marriage when she had had a boyfriend that really liked doing that with her. She closed her eyes tightly and her memories and fantasies and the physical pleasure all began to merge. She felt warm.

She hadn't heard him take off his clothes, she thought, when she felt him hard against her. He held her hips and slowly pushed inside her, letting her adjust to him a little at a time. Suddenly, he was completely inside her. She ignored the sharp pain. Holding her hips more tightly, he moved back and forth. He was deliberate. She was aroused by the sounds she heard herself making. She felt herself rubbing against the arm of the couch. It was intense and so very new. He had texted her details about what he was going to do with her. And he was doing it. She was surprised when she had an orgasm.

He held himself inside her while she did. And then he pulled out of her and helped her to sit back on the couch. He untied her wrists from each other and tied them spread apart on the back of the couch. He moved her legs apart and helped her recline.

"Are you comfortable?"

She nodded. That was when she knew there was a third person in the room. For the first time Claire felt worried, even scared. She wasn't afraid of physical harm, exactly. It was more like the feeling of betrayal and the way her husbands had put their own needs above hers. They had, after all, texted about ménage a trois. Even using the term. But this is a first date, isn't it? She was beginning to think she had been stupid trying to be impulsive and live on the edge taking in new experiences. She had been stupid to trust.

She froze.

She felt thin fingers with long nails gliding through her hair and down across her face. They moved seductively over her skin. She smelled perfume and her fear cautiously disappeared. Her senses were completely alive and she found these female fingers electrified her skin.

The woman caressed her head and stroked her hair; her soft fingers moved over her lips and outlined her mouth. Claire felt the woman's hands holding her chin and brushing the hair from her brow.

This unknown woman's voice was hushed and sexy and whispered that Claire had "such pretty hair."

Claire could feel the woman's urgency growing. Aggressive hands replaced the soft, gliding scrapes of fingernails. These kneading female fingers paid particular attention to the parts of Claire's body that she herself felt were her most feminine parts. She savored feeling the stranger's hands touching her the way only she had ever touched herself. Claire felt the stranger's warm, female mouth kissing her breast and then she felt the man kissing her other one.

The male and female hands moved to Claire's legs. The two touched her. They took turns touching her. Sometimes both of them were inside her at the same time. She felt drunk. She couldn't remember ever having so much physical attention and her body was feeling many things at once.

The woman's hands left her and Claire heard her stand up. She heard her kneel in front of her. For an instant she felt the woman's hair brushing against her legs before she felt the woman's breath against her excited skin. The woman leaned in and began kissing her. No woman had ever done this to her and the difference thrilled her. This woman liked kissing her there and she kissed Claire for a long time while the man touched her breasts. He kissed Claire's neck when she had an orgasm against this woman's mouth.

The man and the woman untied her hands and moved her to the living room floor. The man removed her blindfold.

"Don't you want to return the favor?" She noticed again that pleasant tone making this request, both gentle and commanding.

She opened her eyes. Blinking away the darkness of the scarf, her vision cleared and she saw the woman's legs spread apart in front of her. She was uncomfortable. And for the first time that day, she felt as if she was crossing her line. She was putting someone else's needs ahead of hers. But she didn't want it to show. She quickly convinced herself that it wasn't the same thing. She leaned down and gradually began kissing another woman intimately for the first time. She had always liked the way her fingers tasted when she masturbated. This is the same thing, she told herself.

The woman was beautiful. She was slim, maybe even athletically built. Her body writhed subtly. She moaned as Claire pretended she knew what she was doing. It surprised her when the woman grabbed her head and moved her hips back and forth against her. The woman liked what Claire was doing. And it made Claire feel strong and sexually aggressive that she was having this effect on the beautiful woman.

She had almost forgotten the man who she was originally there to see when he pushed into her again. She couldn't believe she was in the middle of this. She liked the man inside her and having his way with her while she had her way with this mysterious woman whose sounds grew louder and were unusual. She liked him holding her hips tightly, making love to her there, and it was something she had been wanting. She remembered their conversation about it.

All three were becoming very noisy when the woman stood up and disappeared into another room.

Alone with the man, Claire focused on how good it felt. She also couldn't help thinking what her ex-husbands would think. She almost laughed out loud at the thought of telling them both every nuanced detail of what was happening.

The woman reappeared. She was wearing a beige toy and it was sticking out. She laid down on her back in the same spot where she had been a minute before.

The man removed himself and then helped slide Claire on top of the woman's toy. When she was seated the man and the woman moved her hands so that Claire would touch herself as she moved on top of the woman. She felt the toy inside her. And then she felt him inside her too. She was completely filled up.

The two flirted with each other as they fucked their Sunday visitor. She felt used and it aroused her, in spite of herself. She stopped listening to the sounds she heard herself make as they used her to make love to each other. She deliberately shut off her brain and let herself become a sexual object. She let herself give in to the experience.

She was out of breath when the three separated. The mystery woman and Claire together kissed the man's erection. They kissed each other. They took turns putting him in their mouths. The two women's lips were against him when he found release.

Driving home she thought about how nonchalantly she had been able to drink ice tea with the couple after they had sex. She couldn't believe that they had talked about work and people they all knew.

She thought about how casually she embraced it when the three of them had sex again. That time the woman was on top of her. Claire didn't have another orgasm with the couple.

The afternoon hadn't lasted more than a few hours. When just as quickly she had driven home and was showering. In the shower, she found that she just didn't know what to think about what she had let herself do. Wasn't it what she had wanted when she drove over that afternoon?

Before long, memories of that day embarrassed her. She learned that the mysterious woman was a psychologist and that she was engaged to the substitute teacher.

The couple called her several times but she never saw them again. And at school, on days he was substituting, Claire's greeting was cordial.

One Friday Afternoon In a Southern Town

At the top of the landing, a woman sits down at a computer desk and opens Facebook. She clears her password and enters a new one. It opens the profile page that is her daughter's. The house is empty, so it is ok for this mother to do this with her daughter's account. She drinks from the second glass of wine she had poured in the kitchen and, a little cock-eyed, she opens the messenger window, and she reads.

Sunday August 19

Anthony St. George
hey!

Campbell 'C-doll' Hampton
Hey, You!

Anthony St. George
what's going on?

Campbell 'C-doll' Hampton
I just got done watching a sad movie. ☹

Anthony St. George
awww. you've been on a sad movie kick lately, haven't you?

Campbell 'C-doll' Hampton
I have! How did you know?

Anthony St. George
you posted that you saw a sad movie last week.

Campbell 'C-doll' Hampton
You've been spying on my posts!

Anthony St. George
i've been NOTICING your posts. lol

Campbell 'C-doll' Hampton
Aww! You are sweet!

Anthony St. George
☺

Campbell 'C-doll' Hampton
I think you would like this movie. It's sad but tonight I watched it again. It's SO GOOD!!! What are you up to?

Anthony St. George
you watched it again? it must be good…and sad! lol

Campbell 'C-doll' Hampton
Oh it is!

So what's up with you?

Anthony St. George
just chillin at home. its been a crazy day.

Campbell 'C-doll' Hampton
Really? Why? What happened?

Anthony St. George
well, today was my sister-in-law's baby shower. my brother is having a daughter soon. i wasn't even invited but they used me all day today for my cooking skills…then after that they

used my cleaning and dish washing skills…i'm tired

i mean, at least i got to eat some leftovers. ☺

Campbell 'C-doll' Hampton
Leftover clean plates with nothing to eat off of them. Sounds fun! Your sister in law needs to be in the kitchen where she belongs, not you! ☺

Anthony St. George
haha yea, totally fun for me, right?

in her defense….she looks like she's about to pop lol

but my entire family helped with the shower because they couldn't really afford any catering or a planner or anything.

Campbell 'C-doll' Hampton
I think it is sweet that you did all the cooking.

Do I know your sister in law?

Anthony St. George
you might. her name is Amanda and she's in my friends list.

Campbell 'C-doll' Hampton
I see her. She looks nice.

Anthony St. George
oh she is totally cool….most of the time. Lol

Campbell 'C-doll' Hampton
LOL. What else is going on?

Anthony St. George
hmmm. ohh! i just finished school last week!!

Campbell 'C-doll' Hampton
College? That's awesome! Congrats.

Anthony St. George
yes ma'am i am totally done now ☺ and thank you ☺

Campbell 'C-doll' Hampton
What did you graduate as?

Anthony St. George
well my degree is a bachelor's in professional communication. i've already got a job lined up.

Campbell 'C-doll' Hampton
That sounds interesting! What's professional communication?

Anthony St. George
it involves like public relations and advertising and stuff like that. it's an ok job and i will work with the community here. but what about you? what grade are you in?

Campbell 'C-doll' Hampton
Well I doubt you would be okay with my age.

Anthony St. George
uh oh ☹

Campbell 'C-doll' Hampton
LMAO. Or you just wouldn't believe me.

Anthony St. George
i probably won't, i'm terrible at guessing ages. i know how old i think you look...your picture is really hot!!!....but how old are you?

Campbell 'C-doll' Hampton
Well how old do you think? How old are you?

Anthony St. George
i just turned 22 last friday....well i only have one picture to judge by, i can't see your other pics.

you tell me first, and i'll tell you what i would have guessed from your one picture.

Campbell 'C-doll' Hampton
We're just 10 years apart. ☹

Anthony St. George
woah!! you have got to be kidding!!!

Campbell 'C-doll' Hampton
Serious!

Anthony St. George
there is no way!!!!!

god you look like a freaking supermodel in your picture or at least 17-18

now i feel stupid cuz you probably don't want to talk to me

Campbell 'C-doll' Hampton
Of course I want to talk to you! And thank you so much! 18 is the highest guess I've gotten in a while! Usually 17 is what people guess.

Anthony St. George
you want to talk to me still? 10 years is a big difference.

Campbell 'C-doll' Hampton
I'll be twenty soon enough. ☺

Anthony St. George
yeah but that's not for another 8 years lol.

Campbell 'C-doll' Hampton
Remember that they say patience is a virtue.

Anthony St. George
lol. i don't even know what you look like besides that one extremely gorgeous picture ☺

Campbell 'C-doll' Hampton
Well that's because Mr. Smooth 22 over there still hasn't sent me a friend request. ☺

Anthony St. George
ohhh!!! you mean me? ☺

Campbell 'C-doll' Hampton
No, the other hot 22 year old.

Anthony St. George
whoa now! lol you've only seen my one picture also, right?

i sent it btw

Campbell 'C-doll' Hampton
I see all…

Anthony St. George
you did??? i thought my privacy setting only let strangers see my one profile picture?

Campbell 'C-doll' Hampton
Nope. All the creepers are jerking to all of your hot pictures.

Anthony St. George
omg!!! that's sketchy. i am going to fix that NOW!!!

hey campbell…

Campbell 'C-doll' Hampton
Yes?

Anthony St. George
i like talking to you!

Campbell 'C-doll' Hampton
I like talking to you too! ☺☺☺

Anthony St. George
hey campbell…

Campbell 'C-doll' Hampton
Yes?

Anthony St. George
you're making me blush…do you flatter every new guy you meet like this?

Campbell 'C-doll' Hampton
Only the deserving…I'm just speaking truth!

Anthony St. George
you are exceedingly sweet. ❤

Campbell 'C-doll' Hampton
You have an exceptionally vast vocabulary. ❤

Are you related to the Keech family????

Anthony St. George
as do you ☺

and no, i'm not, why?

Campbell 'C-doll' Hampton
I saw that Sarah Keech liked one of your pictures and that Miranda Keech just had a baby. Lol sorry. But I can turn that question into a pick-up line.

Anthony St. George
ohhh haha well i know miranda's dad…i am about to start working with him.

"and no, i'm not, why?" lol go ahead with the pick up line ☺ lol

Campbell 'C-doll' Hampton
Miranda's dad is my preacher! And okay…I'll make up one tomorrow. I haven't slept in 2 days.

Anthony St. George
you go to evan's church? very cool! i've known him for a very long time, he used to be my youth leader

but no!! go on with the line now! i wanna hear it. then get some sleep lol

Campbell 'C-doll' Hampton
Tomorrow, OK? I promise. I have to get up for school in the morning.

Anthony St. George
LOL OK. ☺

goodnight, gorgeous campbell, or is it c-doll? Lol

Campbell 'C-doll' Hampton
I like Campbell. What about you? Is it Anthony or Tony?

Anthony St. George
most everyone calls me anthony.

Campbell 'C-doll' Hampton
I like Anthony. It is very sophisticated!

Although maybe in person I might call you Tony…if no one else is around. ☺

Anthony St. George
it's a deal!!!

Campbell 'C-doll' Hampton
Sweet dreams, Anthony. Xoxoxo

Anthony St. George
sweet dreams, campbell.

campbell?

Campbell 'C-doll' Hampton
Yes, Anthony?

Anthony St. George
I do like talking to you!!!

Campbell 'C-doll' Hampton
☺☺☺

Monday August 20

Campbell 'C-doll' Hampton
Hey, You!!! ☺☺☺

Anthony St. George
hey there!!! you are done with school early!

Campbell 'C-doll' Hampton
Actually, I am still in class. Last period. Boring. There's a sub so I'm chatting with you! ☺

Anthony St. George
☺

i'm still kinda not believing you, you're way too mature looking to be 12...i mean that in the best way possible though, you are beautiful.

Campbell 'C-doll' Hampton
I swear im 12. April 18, 1999. Thank you sooo much, it means a lot.

Anthony St. George
i see you and all i can say is wow. you're basically stunning. ☺

Campbell 'C-doll' Hampton
You're sweet. And what about you? You are basically a model. Your face is perfect for watch advertisements, I swear I'm not kidding.

Anthony St. George
ohh come on! i've never done any of that before.

Campbell 'C-doll' Hampton
You haven't done any modeling? I suggest you get into it.

Anthony St. George
i wouldn't even know where to start.

Campbell 'C-doll' Hampton
I think you would do really well.

Anthony St. George
i think you are just saying that because of the hoody pictures lol

Campbell 'C-doll' Hampton
Lol You are gorgeous. Gush.....

Anthony St. George
blushing big time over here!

Campbell 'C-doll' Hampton
Tell me about it!

What'd you do today?

Anthony St. George
well i woke up around noon did some chores at the house then ran some errands. i just got home.

you still there?

Campbell 'C-doll' Hampton
Sorry. School got out and I got a ride home. I hate the bus. I'm home now.

Anthony St. George
lol

Campbell 'C-doll' Hampton
I am soooo hungry...idk how to do food.

Anthony St. George
you don't know how to do food??? lol awwww i would cook for you love.

Campbell 'C-doll' Hampton
Come over and cook cause I'm starving!

Anthony St. George
i'd love to!
maybe one day i'll be making a homemade meal for ya. where do you live?

Campbell 'C-doll' Hampton
I sure hope so. I'm gonna go beg my brother to drive me to Mcdonalds.

Text me later? <33

Anthony St. George
I can't wait to!

Campbell 'C-doll' Hampton
Be back later. – Me

Anthony St. George
hahahaha ok you!

Campbell 'C-doll' Hampton
Hey, You!

Anthony St. George
There you are!!! That was a long trip to Mcdonalds lol

Campbell 'C-doll' Hampton
LOL I ended up hanging out with my brother and his friends. It was like a lock-in with a bunch of perverts!!!

Anthony St. George
that sounds serious should i be worried?

Campbell 'C-doll' Hampton
LOL No!!! I've known them all forever. They are practically family.

Anthony St. George
lol ok

its late already. you have school tomorrow.

Campbell 'C-doll' Hampton
Yeah. Hold on. brb

Anthony St. George
K

Campbell 'C-doll' Hampton
Back. I wanted to change quick so I can jump into bed.

I'm wearing a new t-shirt and it is sooo soft!

Anthony St. George
i bet it looks amazing on you!!!

Campbell 'C-doll' Hampton
Text me. I'm heading to bed. 8505554433 We can text each other to sleep. I might even show you my new shirt…if you are nice. ☺

Anthony St. George
i'm always nice!

i would be honored to text you baby.

Tuesday August 21

Campbell 'C-doll' Hampton
Hey. You on?

Anthony St. George
yep waiting for you. how'd it go today?

Campbell 'C-doll' Hampton
I was recognized out of 20 students and they picked me to do a solo at the next concert.

Anthony St. George
Omg are you serious?! that's so awesome congrats!! ☺

but that reminds me of something

Campbell 'C-doll' Hampton
What? And thanks so much.

Anthony St. George
you're welcome love! and it reminds me that you didn't listen to me sing last night

Campbell 'C-doll' Hampton
I think someone forgot. They probably got distracted by other things. ☺

Anthony St. George
Ya think?

Campbell 'C-doll' Hampton
I have to go. My mom is calling. Maybe you will remember later?

Anthony St. George
Ok

Campbell 'C-doll' Hampton
Promise to text me later?

Anthony St. George
i will when i get back from the store. i'm making a shopping list right now. and then i'm making pizza.

Campbell 'C-doll' Hampton
Don't forget to put prune juice on that list, grampa! Save me a slice of pizza?

Anthony St. George
i'll definitely save you a slice if you want. my famous pizza.

ohhh! and if you are going out later, don't forget your formula.

Campbell 'C-doll' Hampton
Oh nooo. It's hard to forget my formula, when I'm tired and want my damn crib.

Anthony St. George
hahaaaa you made me laugh! gotta run. <33

Campbell 'C-doll' Hampton
Bye You!

Thursday August 23

Campbell 'C-doll' Hampton
Hey!

Anthony St. George
hey there love

Campbell 'C-doll' Hampton
I didn't hear from you yesterday.

Anthony St. George
i'm sorry. yesterday was pretty crazy.

Campbell 'C-doll' Hampton
Oh no! What happened?

Anthony St. George
well i was supposed to start work this week but my clearance hasn't been granted yet. without that clearance approval i can't work with the ministry. i spent all day running around and checking on paperwork and doing boring stuff.
not gonna lie, i really missed talking to you

Campbell 'C-doll' Hampton
I thought you might not like me anymore. ☺

Anthony St. George
OMG is that even possible?
i think i like you more every minute.

Campbell 'C-doll' Hampton
Good.
My friend came to school high this morning so I had to clean the poor thing up.

Anthony St. George
are you serious?
dangg

Campbell 'C-doll' Hampton
Yeah. Kids are crazy.

Anthony St. George
that's crazy. did she get caught?

(or he?)

Campbell 'C-doll' Hampton
Nope.

Anthony St. George
campbell you know what?

Campbell 'C-doll' Hampton
Hmm?

Anthony St. George
i feel dumb for not getting to meet you at the concert last weekend. i really wanted to. it was before we had talked. i was still getting the nerve to message you.

Campbell 'C-doll' Hampton
I know. I still can't believe we were both at that concert! My mom would of probably freaked out though if you had introduced yourself.

Anthony St. George
why?

Campbell 'C-doll' Hampton
9 years difference. You learned about sex when I was born.

Anthony St. George
We've talked about this before.

Campbell 'C-doll' Hampton
Yeah I knooow

Anthony St. George
this really sucks
why can't i just meet you? ☹

Campbell 'C-doll' Hampton
We will one day.

Anthony St. George
i hope so, but i have a feeling that it's gonna be that one day we meet by accident.

Campbell 'C-doll' Hampton
Accidents happen. Everything happens for a reason. We are talking now aren't we?

Anthony St. George
i mean that i think you and i are supposed to randomly run into each other one day before we can actually plan to meet up. it's just a feeling. who knows. maybe this weekend? ☺

Campbell 'C-doll' Hampton

Good feeling, huh?! I sure hope so. Weird stuff always happens to me when I have a feeling.

Anthony St. George
not so much a feeling, now that you mention it. it's more mathematical. statistically i see the chances of that happening more likely than us planning to meet.

Campbell 'C-doll' Hampton
This sounds scientific.

Anthony St. George
very

Campbell 'C-doll' Hampton
Text me later? I've gtg

Anthony St. George
Ok

Campbell 'C-doll' Hampton
Maybe I'll have a new t shirt to show you and you can mathematically tell me where we might statistically run into each other.

Anthony St. George
you are making me insane for you.

Campbell 'C-doll' Hampton
Isn't that crazy? Bye boo. Behave!

Anthony St. George
ok love.

The mother takes in a mouthful of wine, holds it deliberately, swallows, and types.

Friday August 24

Campbell 'C-doll' Hampton

Hello Anthony,

This is Campbell Hampton's mother.

You have been talking to her on Facebook. She's 12 years old.

You've been making advances.

It's illegal.

You are to defriend her. and you are to defriend every other girl who is underage that you are communicating with.

You are not to contact her again.

If you do contact her again I will be calling the Sheriff.

That won't be good for your job with the ministry and your "clearance".

Do you understand?

The woman hits enter. She watches as the circle with Anthony's face appears next to the new message she's sent to him acknowledging that it has indeed been read by him. She feels more satisfaction than she expected when, within five minutes Anthony's Facebook account disappears. She confirms that Anthony's account has indeed been deleted and that he is not simply blocking her when she logs into severseveral other accounts with other passwords that are not hers, including her husband's. She smiles and exits Facebook.

She swallows her last mouthful of wine and heads downstairs to the kitchen for a refill, taking her time descending the stairs. She is looking forward to telling her girlfriends this story when they meet later at Dumphrey's Beachside Lounge for drinks. She and the girls liked the cover band that played there last Friday. The songs the band played were familiar to them from their high school days and the so the music isn't challenging. They can focus on themselves. The mother looks forward to seeing the cover band's young bass player again. Last week, after the gig, the two of them had enjoyed each other alone behind the sand dunes. Still smiling, she sends her new 23-year-old musician friend a quick text saying as much before disappearing into her bedroom to shower and make herself up for the night out.

An Ass Like Buddy Hackett

This is the damnedest place.

Mom frequently said this.

Mom had been an aide in a nursing home. That was her job. That was where she spent most of her living days. She earned our food and rent caring for those who were too old, too broken, or too confused to care for themselves. So, Mom cared for them, and her days were long. I'm guessing that the residents' days were even longer. Until they died, of course. I imagine being dead is like one long day, whether there is a heaven or not. Sometimes I feel like I am stuck in one long day.

Mom liked sharing stories from Center Village. Center Village is where Mom worked. When I was a kid, she jokingly called it "The Nuthouse" because of all the folks there who had "loose screws". Mom liked saying that, too. It made her smile and Mom had a great big honest smile. One resident was the source of many of Mom's stories. Her name was Alice Purvis and Miss Purvis was old, really old. One of the aides, Annie Jo, was really funny and she used to tell me that Miss Purvis had cooked biscuits for Lee back in Gettysburg. She looked that old to me. I remember. Until I was a teenager it was easy to get transportation around the city and Mom used to bring me to the nursing home with her all the time.

Miss Purvis was mostly blind and mostly deaf, and she never left her bed. She chewed snuff, not chewing tobacco. Snuff. It's gritty, black stuff that looks like gunpowder. It came in a small tin. She would only spit it into a paper cup, and it absolutely had to be a Dixie brand paper cup (paper cups used to be available and Dixie is no longer a word anyone uses). She had a piercing Southern accent, and she directed that voice like artillery toward anyone and everyone passing by her small room.

Miss Purvis would call out, "Can you hep me? Can you? Y'awl listenin'? Anybody? Won't ya hep me please?" And whether anyone answered her or not, Miss Purvis would raise her voice just as much as her 90-pound skeleton allowed and proclaim, "This is the damnedest place," or, the all-inclusive, "This is the damnedest place, and these are the god damnedest people." So, in time, Mom adopted Miss Purvis' phrase for nearly every situation that was even slightly askew. Nowadays things are more than slightly askew. This truly is the damnedest place.

My grandmother had been a nurse. It was what she had wanted to be from the time she was a little girl. Grandma's father, my great-grandfather, had been a successful doctor and his financial success meant that my grandmother had options. In those days there were many places Grandma could go to become a nurse and work as a nurse. Even more importantly, there were places where Grandma could go to learn to be a nurse from other nurses in nursing schools, in person. And so, when the time came, she chose to become a nurse.

My mother, on the other hand, did not have many choices. Things had changed. Options for individual human beings scarcely existed when my mom entered the workforce. By then Mom was only able to find work as a nurse's aide and she learned how to do that on the job, in person. It paid the bills, as I said before, but Mom never told me she worked hard because she was trying to make a better life for me and her. My mom didn't lie. Besides, by the time I was a kid, the virtual world had taken over because the outside world had collapsed.

Nowadays, beyond the basics of food, water, and shelter, there isn't much that can be done with money. More food. More flower. Delivered by drone-bots to your front door. I guess I could buy nice clothes but what is the point? There is nowhere for me to go, and the drone-bots don't care how I look.

When it came time for me to find a job, I had exactly two options. First, I could work at the front door of the building next to the building where I live. The job there was pushing the button that opened the huge, heavy security doors to the building after the face recognition scan was completed and the resident's identity confirmed, or after a drone-bots delivery status is confirmed. It paid enough to cover rent and utilities, and to eat modestly. I would have had plenty of flower to smoke, and there would have been some money left over after that.

That's not the job I picked. I picked the other option---this gig, that I am walking to right now, that I have walked to every day of the week for...I don't really know how many years it has been. Keeping track of the date doesn't make much sense when you've got nowhere to go. I started work when I was 17 and I'm in my 40s now, I guess. Where I work pays much better than front-door-button-pusher but like I said, money doesn't really mean much these days.

Being around real people is the main reason I took this job. I do get to interact with a few other people in the flesh each day, like my friend Bruce. When I started, I had really hoped there might be women working here. Sadly, when they hired me, I replaced the very last woman to have worked here. She had worked until she decided to retire. Her name was Julie H. and she spent the rest of her days with her loving husband, Mr. H., in their apartment, I suppose.

Bruce and I won't be retiring. We'd rather die at our workstations near someone breathing than die in our apartments alone, to rot. The odds are slimmer than slim that we will ever meet anyone to love and to retire with. New people won't move into the area, and no one is making babies that might grow up and work here. It is the way life is now. When we are all dead, the machines in this office will eventually go offline, and the building will become a decaying mausoleum. This is the damnedest place.

I like to read. The virtual world is filled with every kind of book you can think up. Sure, most books were written years ago. I'm not even sure anyone writes anything new anymore. You'd have to have experiences or at least interesting thoughts in order to generate enough content for literature. I doubt anyone nowadays could even generate a decent limerick let alone a novel. Everyone's stuck living inside, and there's only so much inspiration one can get from isolation.

Mostly I read the classics from the 20th Century, Ernest Hemingway, Kurt Vonnegut, Roald Dahl, George Orwell, Sinclair Lewis, and William Faulkner. My favorite author is John Steinbeck. I have read and listened to *Of Mice and Men* dozens of times. These writers all seemed to be warning us not to become what we have become. They hinted and no one listened. Even if they had shouted no one would have listened, I'm guessing.

I have one physical book that I've had since I can remember. I really like the way the pages sound when I turn them. It's a children's picture book and it's called *The Guam ABC's.* My dad was in the Navy overseas, and he brought it back for me right after I was born. Dad was in the Navy because that was his only choice for a job. When I was very young, I remember seeing him three or four times and then, we didn't see him again. I guess Dad at least had some choices that were convenient for him. I don't have any pictures of Dad and I haven't looked for any.

That grey brick wall over there, the one with the rusty razor wire covering it like a crown of thorns replaced the entrance to what was a park way back when. That is the last place I remember being with Dad. He was holding my hand and we were walking through grass that was tall and tickled my legs. I don't remember when the park disappeared, and the wall went up. But I do remember what grass smells like. Geez, I can't remember the last time I saw a real blade of grass.

Here. Let's stop here before I need to go into work. I still have a couple of minutes and I like this concrete bench. This cul-de-sac used to be a bus stop. Sometime after the buses stopped running someone decided to wall off this alley with cinder blocks. Over the years graffiti began appearing until nearly every square inch of the wall was covered. In the mornings before work, and if the rain is not too heavy, I like to back a bowl with flower, light up, and take in all the scribbles and doodles.

I'm not sure I'd call it art. It entertains me. Along the wall there is a lexicon of profanity. There are also a number of eyeballs, some with tears, and a variety of male and female body parts. But what fascinates me most are the messages written clearly and confidently.

Ron Loves Jenny.

Judy Loves Ron.

Go St. Lucius.

Suck it.

Someone wrote, "The End is Near." And someone else crossed out the 'N' and replaced it with an 'R'; "The End is Rear." Funny.

My favorite has always been, "She has an ass like Buddy Hackett." I can't imagine the person who took the time to spray paint that on a wall, but I'd love to meet them and get the full story on that one. I looked up Buddy Hackett and I'm certain that it isn't a compliment for the anonymous 'she' or for Buddy Hackett.

No matter how many times I look at those marks, I am fascinated. Like those caves in Altamira, this graffiti may be the only sign that any of the artists were ever alive.

If you look closely, on the very bottom, far left corner, you can see where Mom and I left our mark. It was a long time ago. The date next to our names was Mom's last birthday and the very last time we took a walk together in the sunshine. In fact, that's also the day when I learned about those remarkable caves in Spain.

Mom told me that those rock paintings are the earliest works of art created by human hands. Those artists left behind vibrant images of deer, buffalo, and horses. They left behind painted handprints. And they left behind symbols that are indecipherable. Even more so than the Buddy Hackett piece. I used to spend a lot of time hanging out in the virtual world version of those caves—most of what I have seen and experienced has been in the virtual world. I don't teleport there anymore but this cinder block wall still amuses me.

I don't know how the world ended up being the way it is. I certainly don't think that there is any one thing that can be blamed for all of this. Besides, even if I did have answers for you, it would be complicated. It would take too long to tell and I need to finish this doobie and head in to work.

I can say this. I have seen countless pictures of the past from archives. I have seen pictures of parks teeming with families taking in the day, children running in grass and playing games, and couples holding hands. Happy faces. But as time passed by the pictures changed into photographs of crowds gathered, separated by barriers, holding signs, and people screaming at each other. Unhappy faces. As the last hundred years rolled by, there were more and more pictures of unhappy faces and fewer and fewer pictures of happy ones. I found lots of pictures of people complaining. Mom once told me that when the laws were written they were designed to protect people from the tyranny of the greedy. But slowly the number of complainers exploded to such a degree that ideas of freedom became so extreme, and the laws so diluted that law no longer made any difference, they stopped protecting, and freedom became our tyranny. That's what Mom said. Mom said, "The dipshits won, Sweetie."

Technology was supposed to help humanity adapt, survive, and thrive. Once upon a time there was the notion that we were destined for the stars. Now our only destinations are virtual worlds created to occupy our time in our residences as the desire to venture forth in the world no longer exists. All our entertainment and most of our human contact is virtual, online. No one ever actually goes anywhere. My walk to work through this polluted, broken glass, concrete, and rusted metal back alley in a city that was used up long ago, is probably the farthest I will ever travel. After 30,000 years, we are more stuck in caves than those hopeful and expressive Paleolithic ancestors. At least I get to hang with Bruce.

OK. This smoke is finished, and I need to head in and start emptying caches and deleting accounts. Yeah. That is my job. Me and Bruce delete the digital vestiges of people that are no longer active. Maybe their creators are dead. Maybe they just got bored. At any rate, nowadays, cleaning the digital world is more important than cleaning up the physical world.

This is the damnedest place.

After Tiramisu and Coffee

They hadn't done it before and afterward she was crying and because he didn't understand why she was crying he didn't know what to say.

When he asked if he had hurt her, she shook her head, no, he hadn't. She shook her head, no, again, when he asked if he had done something wrong. Reasons that might be causing her to cry were rapidly multiplying in his brain. He wrapped his arms completely around her, to hold her close, as he had done many times before. She pulled away from him, curling herself into a ball. She cried quietly in that tight cocoon without saying a word.

That small distance between her body and his made him feel like he was filthy. He wanted to unwrap his arms from her. But there was something about the idea of pulling away from her that seemed inappropriate, wrong. And so, lying next to her, his arms limply draped around her, he remained absolutely still, at the same time trying to and trying not to hold her. She had put on panties and a thick night shirt after it was over but before she slid back into bed and started crying. He was still naked, and it made him feel ashamed.

In the nine months they'd been together, he had never seen her cry. When they met, they connected easily. She was an art student, a painter, and he was studying history. They were both smart and they never ran out of things to say to each other. He'd spent Christmas with her family and a couple of months after that they'd spent a spring break together visiting Big Sur and Monterey as a couple.

This night had been great. They'd gone to their favorite restaurant and after, they had iced coffee and tiramisu at their favorite coffee bar. On the streetcar ride home and sitting very close to him she'd put her head on his shoulder and wrapped her arms around his arm very tightly. He liked feeling her head against him when her eyes were closed.

He had known he was falling in love with her before this night. And when she suggested that they try after they got off the streetcar and went inside her apartment, he was glad he was falling in love with her. But now she was lying there crying and he felt filthy not knowing what to say and not knowing why.

"Are you OK?" *Dumb.*

She was crying.

"What's wrong?"

Almost holding his breath, he waited long minutes for her to answer but she just cried quietly.

"Did something happen?"

He hated not knowing but even more, he hated the feeling that he disgusted her. When her crying softened into sobbing, he tried to hold her close again. She barely moved. Her stiff body reminded him of carrying the plastic nativity statues they had used to decorate the front yard when he was a kid.

"Did something happen?" He didn't know why he asked again.

She had mentioned a couple of boyfriends, and a bad date or two when they were first getting to know each other but she really hadn't gone into many specifics about her past relationships. There had been one boyfriend, from high school, she had been serious about before he had lied to her. Something bad, she had said, but she didn't say more and the look on her face made him feel as if he shouldn't ask her to say more.

He remembered those conversations now, and the high school boyfriend that lied to her about something, and the look on her face when she didn't talk about it. He didn't know why but he felt jealous, and he felt angry for feeling jealous. He wasn't used to feeling angry and jealous. He didn't like it. They felt like a couple at dinner but now it felt like two acquaintances that weren't even friends.

He thought back to when they met and first talked over coffee and tiramisu. She liked his dark, ironic humor from the start, she had said. He liked making her laugh and she laughed easily at his jokes. He wanted to use that ironic sense of humor to lighten the mood now.

"I sure hope I'm not paying the price for someone else's crime. That wouldn't be very nice at all."

It didn't sound like humor when he blurted it out. He sounded mean. It wasn't what he had meant to say at all. He wanted her to see that he was falling in love and that he wasn't going anywhere. But the high school boyfriend and her silence, the jealousy, and suspicions, and what he had just heard himself say to her, left him feeling like he didn't know who he was. He hated what he had said.

I sure hope I'm not paying the price for someone else's crime. That wouldn't be very nice at all.

She didn't respond.

The apartment was pitch black except for the red LED numbers on the alarm clock. He watched the minutes change slowly. Neither of them moved.

Eventually she stopped sobbing and fell asleep, still in that tight cocoon. And after a while, and feeling dumb, he slowly took his arm off of her, and he rolled over and went to sleep.

They never did talk about it. The feeling that he disgusted her was never far from his mind. He never would know what to do or say. Even four years later when they were married and after they tried again and there was no crying after.

The Bell Curve

I drink here. It's the only bar around here anymore like it.

My bar doesn't have a theme or gimmick. There are no trivia nights and no ladies' nights. On the walls hang a few beer signs, a handful of framed and autographed portraits of no one famous, a wall mounted phone that hasn't worked for decades, and the first dollar bill this bar ever made, thumbtacked behind the register and next to the liquor license.

Behind the bar, bottles are lined according to frequency of use. Bourbon, vodka, and gin are up front. Tequila is not allowed in the front row, though it rightly deserves to be. It's in the back row next to a bottle of brandy that has never been cracked. Rum is found in both rows. Below the bar there are coolers filled mostly with bottles of beer. There is no tap, and the only mixers here are tonic, cranberry juice, Coke, and coffee. There is always a cold can of pineapple juice too, the owner's stash, for when he drinks his rum, hidden in the back row on the other side of the brandy bottle.

Inside, along with the bar's ten chairs, there are usually five or six small round wooden and thickly varnished tables, and outside, there are five or six more of those tables, umbrellaed, on a back deck that looks out over the white sand beach and the warm Gulf beyond that.

I've been coming here for a while and it's the only place I ever go anymore, besides the Dollar Store for groceries, and home. It was maybe a year or so after I started drinking that I was staggering along the beach and found this place empty and open on a Christmas Eve. I'm sure I looked like hell's janitor.

I met Jimbo that night. He was kind to me and it reminded me that I had forgotten what kindness looked like.

"Well, Sir, it's Christmas Eve and tradition says we should be drinking brandy." Jimbo poured me a full glass of expensive bourbon and then he poured one for himself.

"You see that bottle of brandy back there by the tequila?" Jimbo spoke to me like we had known each other for years.

I nodded and felt myself smile when I tasted the bourbon. I followed Jimbo's every word.

"I bought this place from a guy named Clinton…he was one of those last-name-first-name guys. Anyway, Clinton told me that the brandy was left over from the original owner. Who knows if that's true. So, out of respect for the tradition we never crack that bottle. No one asks for brandy around here anyway. It's Florida." Jimbo sipped his bourbon, put down his glass, and patted my forearm that was resting on the bar and holding my drink. He put some Christmas music on the TV.

"Ya know…?" He had paused abruptly and was half talking to me and half thinking out loud. He turned and went into the back room and almost immediately he was back at the bar. In both hands he was carrying a small electric grill. He put it at the end of the bar and plugged it in.

"I grew up in New Orleans," Jimbo began. "And my Daddy used to go to this little dive on Magazine Street. Daddy liked to drink; you see. Now he didn't drink all the time but when he did, well, he liked it. So, after a day or so Momma would send me out to collect him and fetch him home. Well, it didn't take much, cuz Daddy was always at that bar on Magazine."

"I'd walk in, I was ten years old. It was dusty, smokey…smelled like a rotten orange floating in vinegar and old beer. Daddy would be sitting at the bar, chain smoking Camel Lights, and talking non-stop with Hector, the owner and only employee. Those two bullshitters would talk back and forth for days, literally, as long as Hector kept pouring."

"When Daddy would see me, he would set me up at the bar next to him. Hector always had a bottle of Abita Root Beer opened and in front of me before I could get comfortable. You see, they knew I was there to get Daddy and end their fun. So, they would delay me with root beer. On the best days, Hector had this little grill behind the bar where he would grill steaks that he served with hashbrowns. He put Tony Chachere's on everything and I loved it. Momma knew she didn't have to worry about dinner those afternoons when Daddy would stagger in the house, me in tow, my mouth and shirt covered in steak grease."
Jimbo smiled, "Tonight, it's Christmas Eve, we are going old school."

The bar filled with meat smoke and in no time at all Jimbo slid a plate with steak and hashbrowns in front of me. He gave me a fork and a knife and filled my bourbon glass. The steak was tough, and it had grit stuck on it from the grill. The hashbrowns were soggy; vegetable oil dripped from each fork full. Everything was overwhelmingly salted. And I devoured it all. Jimbo was barely starting as I was clearing my plate.

He smiled. "How long has it been since you've eaten?"

To be honest, I didn't remember as I had been on quite a

bender. I will say though, that steak and those hashbrowns was the best meal I have ever eaten, or probably will ever eat. And that is how I found this place and met Jimbo, and that is why this is the only bar I know anymore. It's been at least 15 years now. I stopped keeping track. When I started, most of my drinking was at home, alone. Occasionally I'd stagger up and down the beach so I could have a smoke. Like I said, that's what I was doing on that Christmas Eve.

Yes. I started drinking. I made the choice. It was May 19th, my birthday. I bought a bottle of bourbon, poured myself a drink, got drunk, and decided that's where I would stay. It's not something that makes sense to most people. But humanity is a Bell Curve and there are some of us who understand, who know, why alcoholism would be a choice.

I'm not saying I'm an alcoholic. I'm not saying I am not one either. Drinking is what I choose to do and it is the only thing I choose to do anymore. And since I have no one who counts on me, I can make the choice to drink without any real consequences.

My parents didn't drink, aside from the occasional glass of holiday wine. I got drunk a couple of times in high school. And in college I was in a fraternity and so I drank quite a bit at quite a few parties. But I was a pothead. I spent most of my time smoking pot. In my 20s and 30s I barely had one drink a month, on average. In my 40s I averaged maybe four or five drinks a month. And that was pretty much how it was until I turned 55 and closed the books, or opened the book, depending on your perspective and sense of humor.

My mom died from cancer when I was 53. I took care of her until the end. I watched her take her last breath. She left the house to me, and I have only a few bills, I buy food and pay for water and electricity. Forget about TV or internet. I just don't care what the rest of the world is doing. I get a check each month now, and I can eat and sleep and drink.

This wasn't what I wanted. I have a bachelor's in English from Stanford, a master's from Vanderbilt. I wanted to teach at a college and be a writer. I wanted to write plays for the drama department. I wanted to publish non-fiction works about Hemingway and Vonnegut. I wanted to write short stories and novels. I wanted to live a quiet suburban life with a wife who loved me. Together we would frequent lectures and recitals and concerts and gallery openings and the theater. And I'd lecture and I'd travel with the wife who loved me.

That didn't happen. Remember the Bell Curve paradigm?

After graduate school I worked on an online literary magazine as a writer and editor. I was married then and teaching as an adjunct at the city college. It turned out my wife didn't care much for literature, my writing, or for me and so after the magazine failed miserably, my wife left me, and I ended up in Florida living with Mom just after Dad died. After ten years at the local community college, I was down to teaching one class of Introduction to American Literature a semester. When Mom got sick, I hardly noticed the loss of pay when I stopped teaching altogether so that I could take care of her.

Something changed profoundly inside me, though, after Mom died. And, as I said before, I watched her take her last breath. Before she was gone, I had resented the education that I had gotten and that couldn't help me find a sustainable career. I resented the country that no longer cared for literature and thus no longer wanted full-time college professors. I resented the technology that made it easy to be published and impossible to get paid for it. I resented the wasted time and the wasted love that went nowhere for indifferent women. And I resented that my parents never had the chance to be proud of me for my accomplishments. I resented the artist inside me with all that ambition. And most of all I resented the Bell Curve that distributed me here. When Mom died, all of the anger that I had been carrying around became so great it simply vanished. And I was free to drink.

It didn't take long before I was drinking all the time. I wasn't necessarily drunk all the time, but I was always drinking. It wasn't hard. I was seldom hung over and I had a gift for never running out of drink. I was already an experienced drunk, and good at it, that Christmas Eve I met Jimbo.

They say an insane person will keep doing the same things while expecting a different outcome. Everyone here in my section of the Bell Curve agrees. I didn't give up. I simply stopped trying to be anything. I retired. I accepted my assigned deviation inside the Bell Curve. I embraced my one truth, that thing upon which I can hang my existential hat until I take my last breath in the same house where Mom took hers: All of humanity is born to achieve. Bell Curves don't care.

Still Life With Lobster

Life was busy on the ocean floor. The relentless ebb and flow of the tides, the ever-changing seasons and their ever-changing currents, created an ocean in constant flux. When you include the passing ships that churned up the water and left their own unpleasant wakes, from small skiffs to giant tankers, it became a difficult proposition to maintain a true direction if you were one of many creatures who lived below. If one wasn't careful one could get lost following the wrong school. Or, even worse, swept out to sea by a rogue wave.

Yes. Life was busy on the ocean floor. And no one felt that more than the Lobster. Lobster walked from side to side and his life was made all the busier by everyone constantly pointing out his fault for not moving forward.

"It must have been his parents," the Sponges were especially fond of saying. "Such deformities are inherited from the parents and so it does no good to notice."

The Octopus was more pragmatic. "Yes. I will have to agree with that. His parents are the source of this problem. Except that it can be helped and it should be noticed. He does no better because his parents taught him to walk; he simply copied their manner. It is our responsibility to rehabilitate him. Although, it could take many seasons."

"That little shit doesn't know what's good for him. He's lazy. He needs to be disciplined." The Shark had very little use for and almost no patience with the Lobster. Discipline dictated cutting through the water with presence and purpose. The Shark had no time for sidestepping across the floor foolishly.

One of the mollusks liked the Lobster even though he could never understand him. "What is it, Lobster? Why won't you learn to move about properly?"

"Because this is the way I move."

"Can't you see that you don't understand why being able to move ahead is better because you have never tried it? You can't see yourself from our perspective. You are impaired."

"Yes, but have you seen it from my perspective? How can any of you? I move from side to side." Lobster never got mad at Mollusk. He never really became angry with anyone, but he could become frustrated.

The Mollusk looked troubled. "Lobster, we all move from side to side sometimes. But we go forward. Don't you see? You are limiting yourself from your potential. You cannot truly be free until you can move forward."

The Lobster did not blink and looked straight ahead. He spoke with clarity and in a monotone voice, as if he were reciting a poem he had recited only too often. "The Shark must keep moving or he will suffocate. The Sponge, though he has a firm foundation, will eventually be harvested. Octopus will be caught in a net if Shark does not catch him first. Even you dear Mollusk, are not completely safe from the hands of a diver. Why am I the only one who is not free? Because I move sideways?"

"No. We won't live forever. But you can do whatever you want with the time you have...don't create more problems for yourself. You could have achievements. Achievements!" Mollusk pleaded as Lobster sidestepped away.

Lobster often wondered what it might be like to have always been able to walk and see where he was going. But then he would think about all that he would have to give up. What fun is it to have a clear view of where you are headed? For Lobster, every day was a new adventure. He liked to guess what he might sidestep into next and, even though he was usually wrong, it was truly thrilling. If you can't move forward you can't go in reverse either. Besides, if achievements are so great, everyone would have them. Lobster's logic was sound.

"Hey Lobster! Man, you are wasting your time. When you gonna wake-up? Probably never." The Seahorse bugged Lobster, and always when he was deep in thought. Seahorse seemed to creep up on him from out of nowhere.

"Gotta ride!" He always yelled the same thing in Lobster's ear and then galloped off.

The Manta Ray had had an appealing idea. "Your claws get in the way. Why don't you use them to your advantage and learn to fly with them?" The Manta Ray was beautiful flying about with such grace.

Lobster was not sure he wanted grace. He liked having big red claws. He admitted that at times he regretted letting them grow so large but, his claws were what made him a lobster. Someone had to be the Lobster; why wasn't anyone satisfied with letting him be the Lobster, with big red claws walking always sideways across the ocean floor?

It was during a high tide that the Lobster was thinking just these thoughts and favoring the left–some days he only walked left and other days he only went right, depending on his mood–when he felt his shoulder pressing against something which he had never felt before. It excited him and he tried to guess what it was. He pressed a little harder with his shoulder.

“I know it isn’t a tire,” he said. He knew tires all too well. He had named them.

He pushed against the *something* harder. He knew that the weight of his body with its awkward center of gravity being forced against the object would eventually spin him around to face the new obstacle.

Suddenly there was a little movement and then a little more. He took heart and pushed harder. Nothing moved and then at once the object gave way and Lobster felt himself turning rapidly in a cloud of sediment into the *something*. He was ready for it to clear. He was already beginning to think of a name to call this *something* when he started to make out a shape.

A few tides later a school of mullet watched as Lobster was pulled through the ocean surface in a wooden crate. And it wasn’t long before the word about the Lobster had gotten around.

Soon, everyone who was interested and some who weren’t, gathered at a sunken fishing boat to pay their last respects. The Eel gave a short eulogy while most of the schools shook their heads in disbelief and pity.

“His was doomed from the start and rocked with resentment all the way," the Eel slithered. The water seemed to stand still and the schools, solemn, barely moving, looked on.

"May the turbulent waters of a turbulent soul find lasting peace in that good, good harbor,” Eel said.

A grouper laughed at the congregation and commented that Lobster was "a victim of his own stupidity of which he supplied the condition for." Nothing phased the Grouper and big tears of laughter rolled from behind his thick glasses and over his pudgy cheeks. Anyone who knew the Grouper could tell you that he thought most everything was really just part of a big joke.

The parrot fish, who didn't eat good but were pretty as pink coral, cackled loudly amongst themselves.

"Dat Lobstah wuz quick to go, wuzn't he?"

"It serve 'im right, lazy fish."

"He got wot come to 'im, always knockin' about like dat."

Almost everyone thought about what the Lobster had wasted and what they all agreed that they were not wasting. Only a wandering crab who happened by the gathering felt any sense of tragedy. He did not tell the others and sidestepped away.

Once In a Broken Rain

Once in a broken rain I thought of you.
I resented those little fingers scraping their nails
    against my face
Like shards from a shattered shot glass I remember
    hurling against a wall.
Stinging instantly, disbelief in the reflected bits.
It is an unseemly universe that dares to dare
    and dare and dare.

Numbed with cold I walked on
Pulling tightly the discount store parka as best I could.